WHAT THE
HEART KNOWS

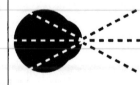This Large Print Book carries the
Seal of Approval of N.A.V.H.

WHAT THE HEART KNOWS

MARGARET DALEY

Thorndike Press • Waterville, Maine

Published in 2004 by arrangement with Harlequin Books S.A.

Thorndike Press® Large Print Christian Fiction.

The tree indicium is a trademark of Thorndike Press.

The text of this Large Print edition is unabridged.
Other aspects of the book may vary from the original edition.

Set in 16 pt. Plantin by Al Chase.

Printed in the United States on permanent paper.

Library of Congress Cataloging-in-Publication Data

Daley, Margaret.
    What the heart knows / Margaret Daley.
      p. cm.
    ISBN 0-7862-6955-3 (lg. print : hc : alk. paper)
    1. Widows — Fiction.   2. Widowers — Fiction.   3. Large
  type books.   I. Title.
  PS3604.A36W47 2004
    813′.6—dc22   2004056337

To Helen Moore,
a friend who has stuck by me through the
bad and good. Friendship is so important,
and I have been blessed with good friends.

As the Founder/CEO of NAVH, the only national health agency solely devoted to those who, although not totally blind, have an eye disease which could lead to serious visual impairment, I am pleased to recognize Thorndike Press★ as one of the leading publishers in the large print field.

Founded in 1954 in San Francisco to prepare large print textbooks for partially seeing children, NAVH became the pioneer and standard setting agency in the preparation of large type.

Today, those publishers who meet our standards carry the prestigious "Seal of Approval" indicating high quality large print. We are delighted that Thorndike Press is one of the publishers whose titles meet these standards. We are also pleased to recognize the significant contribution Thorndike Press is making in this important and growing field.

Lorraine H. Marchi, L.H.D.
Founder/CEO
NAVH

★ Thorndike Press encompasses the following imprints: Thorndike, Wheeler, Walker and Large Print Press.

Thou art my hiding place and my shield:
I hope in Thy word.
Uphold me according unto Thy word,
that I may live:
and let me not be ashamed of my hope.
— *Psalms* 119:114, 116

CHAPTER ONE

Through the crowd packed into the church's recreational hall, Kathleen Somers searched for her sister and nephew. She spied Laura waving from the front row. Quickly Kathleen hurried toward her, aware the talent show would be starting soon.

"I didn't think you were coming. You're never late." Laura indicated she sit between herself and a young girl who looked familiar.

"I didn't think Mark would ever get ready. He wanted to do this, but the way he was dragging his feet you would think I had made him." Kathleen took her seat, smiling at the child next to her.

Laura leaned close and whispered, "Still having problems with Mark?"

Kathleen nodded, not wanting to discuss Mark and his odd behavior of late. Being sixteen was a difficult time in a person's life, but the problems she was having with her son were going beyond adolescent rebellion.

The lights in the hall flashed off then on. The young girl next to Kathleen twisted around in her chair, scanning the back of the room. She knitted her brows together in a frown.

"Is something wrong?" Kathleen asked.

"Dad should be back by now."

"Where did he go?"

She turned back around and peered at Kathleen. "Looking for my brother. You're Chad's aunt, aren't you?"

"Yes, I'm Kathleen Somers."

"I'm Hannah Matthews."

So that was why she looked familiar. Kathleen was acquainted with her father, Dr. Jared Matthews. He took care of her sister's children and was an active member of her family's church.

"Didn't you just move here?" Hannah asked. "Chad said something about helping you move into a house a few weeks back."

"Yes, but I grew up in Crystal Springs, not that many years ago."

"Like me."

"Yeah. I went to Alcott Elementary and Morton Junior High."

"I went to Alcott Elementary, and Morton Junior High is now Morton Middle School. That's where I go."

"Is Mrs. Brenner still teaching Home Economics?"

Hannah's eyes grew round. "Oh, my gosh, yes! Isn't she ancient?"

"She was when I was attending school. I can't believe she hasn't retired."

"I think she'll still be there when the school is condemned," Hannah said with a giggle.

Dr. Jared Matthews approached them, a young boy about eight with dark blond hair at his side. Jared nodded a greeting, his blue eyes warm with a smile. "It's good to see you again, Kathleen. Your return has been all your family has talked about for weeks." He took the seat next to Hannah, his son plopping down next to him with a pout on his face and his arms folded over his chest. "Thank goodness I found Terry in the nick of time."

"What happened?" Kathleen asked, marveling at how much Jared's son looked like him, except for the hair color.

"Let's just say Terry was being a little too enthusiastic in showing his appreciation for his sister."

"Dad, what did Terry do?" Exasperation laced each word.

"He was writing your name on the barrel in the playground."

Terry leaned around his dad, sticking his tongue out at Hannah. "Yeah, with Dylan's."

"Dylan?" The girl's face screwed up into a frown.

"I saw you two talking earlier." Terry began to chant, "Hannah and Dylan sitting in a tree. K-I-S-S-I-N-G. First —"

"Dad!"

Everyone in the recreational hall heard Hannah's protest. Kathleen noticed a few people shift their attention to the girl.

Jared's face turned red for a few seconds, his eyes round. "We can always leave if you two don't settle down."

Kathleen was amazed by Jared's calm tone. His quiet voice held a firmness, however, that promptly communicated his message to Terry and Hannah. Her sister had told her he was good with children. Kathleen had to agree. She wished she felt that way about her relationship with her son. There was a time when she and Mark had been extremely close. Now she found it hard even to carry on a conversation with him. What had happened these past six months to change everything? Was he just being a typical teenager?

"See why I sit between these two?" Jared said, catching her attention. "There are

12

times I think they live to fight with each other."

"You should have seen Laura and me when we were growing up. We used to drive our parents crazy." The lights in the hall dimmed again. "Too bad they're on vacation. They'll hate missing my son's performance. They haven't seen him play in a while."

"I didn't realize he was one of the performers. This will be a treat for us." Jared settled back to enjoy the show as the curtains opened on the first act.

Mark appeared on stage after the fifth act. Kathleen shifted in the seat, crossing and uncrossing her legs. He sat on a stool in front of the mike and adjusted its height, then began to play the Beatles' song, "Yesterday." With his gaze fixed on the floor, he made it through the first verse with not one mistake. A constriction in Kathleen's chest lessened as her son continued playing. Even though he didn't look at the audience, she saw a glimpse of the old Mark on stage.

Halfway through the second verse Mark stopped playing and shot to his feet. He stared at the people at the back of the recreational hall, his posture ramrod straight as though he would break any second. Silence, thick and heavy, reigned. Transfixed,

Kathleen held her breath.

Suddenly Mark raised his Les Paul guitar and smashed it against the floor. Once. Twice. Several people gasped. Mark tossed the fragments toward the back curtain, then spun about and raced from the stage.

Breathe, Kathleen's mind commanded. She sucked in a deep gulp of air and nearly choked. Her heart pounded against her chest while she continued to draw air into her lungs between coughs. The empty stage and the unearthly silence hammered home what had just happened with her son.

Then all at once people began to talk around her, their voices bombarding her from every side. She had to get to Mark. Bolting to her feet, her chair toppling over, she hurried after her son, faintly aware someone was following her flight from the room.

She scanned the long hall leading to the classrooms. Nothing. The outside door beckoned. She moved toward it. Her sister called out.

Kathleen pivoted. "Please go reassure everyone. I can take care of finding Mark."

Laura started to say something.

"I'm fine. I'm sure Mark raised a few eyebrows."

Laura headed back into the recreational

hall, leaving Kathleen alone in the lobby. She fought the desire to call her sister back, but Laura was very good at making a situation not seem so bad and she was sure many people had questions about what just happened. *She* had questions.

Kathleen pushed through the double doors. Heat still hung in the air. Bright oranges and reds streaked the sky, proclaiming a beautiful sunset. Kathleen turned away from its beauty and searched the parking lot. The beating of her heart thundered in her ears, drowning out all sounds of traffic on the road.

Where was Mark? She thought for sure he would be standing by their car. He wasn't anywhere in sight. Panic gnawed at her insides. She remembered the time he had run away a few months back in Shreveport. It had only been for a day, but —

"Kathleen?"

A hand clasped her shoulder. She twisted about to find Jared Matthews standing right behind her. "I can't find him!"

"I'll help you look. He couldn't have gone far. Maybe he's still in the building."

Stepping back, she shook her head. "I don't think so. I —" Words lumped in her throat. Tears misted her eyes, blurring her view of Jared.

He came to her side and placed a comforting hand on her arm. "It'll be all right. I'll look in the parking lot and that area beyond. You search the playground and garden. Okay?"

She brushed away a tear that slid down her cheek. "Yes."

Kathleen hurried toward the playground, suddenly remembering the times her son used to love playing on a jungle gym or swinging on a swing as high as he could go. Years ago. Had she lost him? Why would he smash his Les Paul guitar? He loved it. It had been her son's most prized possession, cherished even more because it was one of the last things his father had given him before he'd died. It had been John's guitar when he was growing up.

A deserted playground greeted her. The wind stirred a flag but that was all that moved. When she started for the garden, she caught a glimpse of the barrel that Terry had written on. The sight of Hannah and Dylan's names brought a faint smile to her mouth that hovered for a second then vanished. She pressed on, wishing she had the time for something frivolous.

In the middle of the garden of tall pine trees from past parishioners' Christmases, Kathleen located Mark sitting on the

16

ground, propped against a stone bench. He clasped his knees to his chest and stared, unblinking, at a spot a few feet from him.

"Mark?"

He didn't move.

Kathleen knelt down in front of him and blocked his view, forcing him to look at her. "Mark, what happened back there?"

"I don't want to play anymore."

There wasn't any emotion in his voice or on his face. The sight made Kathleen shudder. He slid his gaze from hers, again finding a spot to the side of her to stare at. Icy tentacles burrowed deep inside her. Even though the temperature hovered in the eighties, she hugged her arms to her. So cold.

"Mark, you don't have to play music if you don't want to."

"I want to go home." He uncurled himself and pushed to his feet, his movements jerky.

Kathleen rose, taking that time to school her features into a calm facade that was no indication of what she was really feeling inside — fear, fear that she was losing her son, fear that something was going on beyond teenage rebellion. "I think you should see someone about —"

He whirled on her. "No! I told you no doctors." Anger lined his face, his heavy dark brows slashed downward. "I'm fine.

There's nothing wrong with me. I don't want to play. That is all."

"But you destroyed your guitar, the one your father gave you."

"It's *my* guitar. I can do what I want with it."

Again his expression smoothed into a bland one. For a fleeting moment Kathleen wondered if she had imagined her son's anger. Now he looked as though nothing had happened in the recreational hall, as if every day he smashed his favorite things.

"Mark, please let me help you."

He stiffened, pressing his lips together, but his expression remained neutral.

She thought of Mark at his father's funeral, supporting her through the ordeal. All Kathleen wanted to do was pull her son into her arms and hold him. She ached with the need, but his rigid stance forbade it. What had she done wrong that she couldn't reach her son when he needed her the most?

Footsteps sounding on the stone path drew her attention. Jared approached from the parking lot.

Mark stared at him. "I'm going to the car." He rushed past her and Jared.

Kathleen started forward.

"Wait. Give him a moment."

"Why? He —"

Jared stepped in front of her, blocking her path. "*You* need it."

The tight rein she had on her composure broke. Tears streamed down her face, unchecked. She couldn't seem to stop them. She rarely cried, and now she was crying in front of a practical stranger. "I don't know what to do anymore." She paused, inhaling deeply. "These past six months have been so difficult. He's not sleeping like he used to. He often roams the house at night. He's not eating well, either. In fact, this past week I've hardly seen him eating at all. Last night I saw him crying during a movie that was funny." Swiping at her tears, she hiccuped.

His eyes showing his concern, Jared lifted his hand toward her but stopped. Instead he removed his handkerchief from his pocket and gave it to her. "It could be any number of things. I can run some tests and see what I find. Call the office Monday and set up an appointment."

"That's the problem. When I tried to get him to see his doctor in Shreveport, Mark refused. He disappeared the day I was going to take him to the doctor. Talk about a scare." Kathleen raked her trembling fingers through her hair. "I even said something a few days ago about finding a new doctor in town and he stomped from the room, muttering he didn't need one."

"How does your son feel about the move to Crystal Springs? Could his recent change in behavior be because of it?"

She shook her head, brushing the cotton handkerchief across her cheeks, trying to remove all evidence of her lost composure. "We had a long talk before we moved and he told me he didn't care one way or another. The last few months in Shreveport he didn't do much with any of his friends." She peered away, unsure of anything concerning her son of late. "I suppose it could be. I didn't think he minded."

"I understand from your sister your husband died not long ago?"

"Eighteen months."

"His death was sudden, wasn't it?"

"An accident at work. At first, I thought Mark's unusual behavior might be because of his close relationship to his dad, but now I don't know. I know teens can be moody and difficult, but I think this is more than that."

"You might be right. If he won't come in, I'm not sure what I can —" His eyes brightening, Jared snapped his fingers. "No, I have an idea. I'm the director of the youth group. Maybe if you can get him involved in the group, I can observe him indirectly. That might be a start."

"I know his cousin is part of the youth group. I might be able to get him to attend a meeting. After that, I don't know." After wiping her face one last time, Kathleen balled the handkerchief in her fist, then stuffed it into her pants' pocket to clean later.

"There's a meeting Sunday evening. Maybe if he gets to know me, he'll feel more comfortable with coming to see me."

"As you can see, I don't have many choices. I'm willing to try anything," she murmured, for once feeling a ray of hope. Maybe that was the answer.

"I'll walk you to the car. I'll say something to Mark about the meeting Sunday evening."

"He used to be very involved in the youth group in Shreveport until a few months ago. I hope you can convince him to come."

"If not, I'll think of something." Jared fell into step next to her on the stone path leading to the parking lot.

"Frankly, where my son is concerned, I don't know what to think anymore. Right after his father died he was so strong. He was a wonderful comfort to me." Guilt wove its way through all the other feelings she was dealing with. Everywhere she'd gone in Shreveport, she'd been reminded of her deceased husband. All her friends had been John's friends, as well. It had just gotten too painful for her to stay. She'd longed to be around her family; to renew the feeling of belonging she'd had when she'd lived in Crystal Springs as a child. Had she been wrong to leave Shreveport and her old life behind? To want some control back in her life? Had she driven her son to this behavior?

At the edge of the parking lot Kathleen glanced toward her silver Taurus, relieved to see Mark leaning against its hood with his arms crossed over his chest and his shoulders hunched. "For a while he talked to his school counselor, but even that stopped six months ago."

"Let me see what I can do."

She paused two rows away from her car and faced Jared. "My sister has a great deal of faith in your ability. I can't tell you how much I appreciate your help."

He offered her a reassuring smile that brightened his blue eyes. "The reason I became a doctor was because I wanted to help others when they were in trouble. Mark is in trouble. If there is a medical reason, I want to find it and make things better for him. If there isn't a physical reason for his behavior, I still may be able to help him. I have to try."

There was a touch of desperation in his last sentence that caused Kathleen to wonder what had put it there. She wished she knew him well enough to ask. "Thank you for being here."

"You don't need to thank me. It was the right thing to do."

Dressed in a long-sleeved blue chambray shirt and tan slacks, Jared presented a confidence that gave her hope his plan might actually work. Observing Mark interacting with others and his environment was a start. She would continue to encourage her son to go to the doctor for a checkup, but without his cooperation she doubted it would work. "Not everyone would care," she murmured, realizing this man had chosen to get involved in her and her son's life when a lot of people, having witnessed what happened on stage, would run the other way.

"But that's not what Christ taught us."

Kathleen started to reply when she heard, "Mom. Come on."

Shrugging, she said, "I'd better go."

Jared followed her the rest of the way and offered his hand to Mark while he introduced himself. Her son limply shook it, his fingers barely touching Jared's.

"I'd love to see you at the youth group meeting this Sunday evening. You probably know some of the guys who attend. Your cousin is one of our leaders."

Mark avoided eye contact with Jared. "I don't know if I can make it," Mark mumbled to his chest.

"We're going to plan a fundraiser, then continue our volleyball tournament. I can always pick you up if you want or you can come with your cousin. What do you say, Mark?"

Kathleen marveled at the persuasive tone in Jared's voice and hoped her son agreed.

"I'll think about it," Mark mumbled, this time lifting his head and looking Jared in the eye for a few seconds before dropping his gaze again.

"Good. Summer around here can get long and boring without some things to do."

Mark yanked the door open. "Let's go, Mom."

Over the top of the car Kathleen mouthed, "Thank you," then slid behind the steering wheel.

After pulling out of the parking lot, Kathleen stopped at the corner and studied her son's slumped posture and sullen expression. "I can take you if you want

Sunday evening." Her son had refused to get his driver's license three months ago when he'd turned sixteen.

With his gaze glued straight ahead, Mark tensed. "I said I'd think about it."

Kathleen eased her foot onto the accelerator and maneuvered the car out into the flow of traffic. At least her son hadn't flatout refused. There was hope. In fact, because of Jared Matthews she felt more hope than she had in a long time. Maybe this move home was going to turn out for the better after all. She needed to believe in something again. After John's death she had lost faith, her prayers had gone unanswered. Then the recent events concerning Mark had found her drifting even further away from God.

Parking in her driveway, she curled her fingers tightly around the steering wheel and watched her son's quick escape into the house. "I am not alone. I have my family here and someone who may be able to give me some insight into what's going on with my son." The words whispered in the quiet confines of the car reassured her for a moment until she saw her son come to his bedroom window and lower the black shade he'd insisted on having.

Lately Mark preferred to live in the dark,

but she wouldn't. No matter how much she wanted to do everything on her own, she couldn't refuse help — not now when her son's health was at stake. If she had an ounce of strength left in her, she would discover with Jared's assistance what was wrong with Mark.

CHAPTER TWO

Kathleen sat at her table in the kitchen looking out her bay window into the backyard. A green blanket of lush grass extended to a rock garden where a stone bench and birdbath beckoned. Watching a male cardinal land on a branch of her maple tree, she thought about her encounter the night before at the church with Dr. Jared Matthews. There was a presence about him that gave her some hope he might succeed where she hadn't been able to with her son. Maybe he would be able to reach Mark.

As she brought the cup of hot tea to her lips, the doorbell rang, startling her from her musings. She checked the clock on the wall and noticed it was still early in the morning — eight. Quickly, before the person rang the bell again, she hurried to the door. Mark hadn't been asleep long and she didn't want anyone waking him up. He had been so tired after the talent show, and yet she'd heard him roaming around until a few hours ago.

When she opened the front door, she

blinked several times, surprised to find Jared Matthews standing on her porch, his chest rising and falling rapidly.

Dressed in navy blue running shorts and a white T-shirt, he smiled, dimpling both cheeks. Sweat glistened on his brow and dampened his shirt. "I was on my way home from jogging in the park and thought since I wasn't too far from you I would stop by and see how Mark is doing after last night."

"He's asleep right now. Would you like something to drink? Water? Coffee? Tea? I was having a cup of hot tea, but I can fix you some coffee if you like."

Shaking his head, he swiped the back of his hand across his forehead. "Anything hot right now doesn't sound too appealing, but I'll take a tall glass of ice water."

She stepped to the side. "Come in."

He didn't move. "I've been jogging."

She laughed. "Believe me, my kitchen table has seen worse than a man who's been jogging sitting at it."

He opened the screen door and came into the house, his large frame filling the small entry hall. He took a deep breath. "Something smells good."

"I'm baking bread."

"Baking bread? People still do that?"

"I'd do it even if I didn't like to eat it just for the smell."

"My mom used to bake bread, but that was ages ago. I haven't had freshly made bread since I was a young kid."

"I have one loaf finished. I'll cut you a piece if you want."

"There's no way I'll turn down that offer." His smile grew, deepening the two dimples in his cheeks. "This is my lucky morning."

Jared trailed her into the kitchen and took a seat at the glass table. She brought him some ice water, then returned to the counter to cut several slices of bread.

"Do you like to cook?"

She glanced over her shoulder. "Yes. You could call it one of my passions."

"One?" He arched a brow. "What other passions do you have?"

The question caused her to pause. Tilting her head, she thought about it, realizing so many of her passions had been tied up with John. They had loved to hike and camp as a family. They had taken pride in fixing up their old house room by room until it had been stamped with their personalities throughout. "You know, besides cooking, I suppose I like to read just about any type of book."

"You don't sound very convinced."

"So many things that I used to do were connected with my husband and son. Since my husband's death there's been a void that's been hard to fill." Kathleen finished slicing the bread, then brought the plate to the table and sat. "You probably know what I mean. Didn't your wife die recently?"

A slight tensing of the shoulders and clenching of the jaw were the only indication Jared was bothered by her question. He took a sip of his water and picked up a piece of warm bread. "Alice has been gone for a little over a year."

"Then you know how hard it can be to start a new life."

"Yes," he clipped out, downing half his water in several gulps.

"I married John when I was twenty. I've never had a career and I don't have to work now. But suddenly I'm finding my life isn't fulfilling, the way it was when my family was whole. I still take care of Mark and the house, but everything has changed. It's as though I'm at sea adrift with no place to go."

"Have you thought about getting a job?"

Kathleen nodded. "But with the way Mark's been behaving lately, I don't think I should. Maybe if things are better when he starts school in two months, I'll try to find something to do."

"You can always volunteer. We could use someone to organize volunteers at our hospital. Or I could always use an extra person to help with the youth group at church."

Kathleen sipped her lukewarm orange-spice tea. "I'll think about that. I used to volunteer at Mark's school in Shreveport, as well as at our church. I enjoyed doing both of those jobs. If I'd finished college, I probably would have gone into a career as a social worker or a teacher. I like working with people, helping them."

"That's one of the reasons I became a doctor. I suppose you could say fixing problems is a passion of mine."

"Since I have a problem, I'm glad it is."

Jared settled back in his chair, relaxing totally as his gaze shifted to the large bay window. "Your yard is beautiful."

"I wish I could take credit, but the former owners must have loved yard work. They did a wonderful job landscaping. I like to drink my tea in the morning and look outside or sit on the deck if it's not too hot. There's something about a rock garden that's soothing."

"The Hendersons, who owned this house, often worked wonders with the church garden. That'll be a void we'll have to fill."

Kathleen chuckled. "Don't look at me. If I can't find someone to do my yard, this may be the best you'll see."

"Actually I was thinking of taking over that job at the church. I love to work in the yard, get my hands dirty. One of my favorite things is to commune with nature."

"I love to commune with nature, too, like a connoisseur who appreciates fine art but doesn't actually paint." Their gazes connected, forming a momentary bond between them. "But I haven't done any communing with nature lately. John, Mark and I would go out —" Her voice trailed off into silence. That life was over. She had to move on — quit thinking about the past.

"Go where?" Jared asked, his gaze returning to the yard, breaking the bond.

She flattened her back against the chair, the wooden slats pressing into her. "Camping and hiking. Also on trips into the bayous." A long time ago, she thought. She'd come home to start a new life.

"With snakes and alligators?"

"Yes."

"I'm impressed. I could never get my wife to go anywhere outdoors with Hannah, Terry and me."

"She didn't like being outside?"

"No."

Again a shutter fell over his features, clearly putting an end to the direction of the conversation. A finely honed tension sprung up between them. The atmosphere shifted, and she wished the past had remained in the past. Each was uncomfortable talking about their deceased spouses.

Silence prevailed while Jared popped the last bite of bread into his mouth, then finished his water.

"How long have you lived in Crystal Springs?" Kathleen asked, needing the conversation to head in a more neutral direction.

"Ten years. My wife wanted to live near her mother. What made you move back home?"

"My family." My need to put down roots in a familiar place, she added silently. To control the direction my life is taking.

"Family is important."

"I'm hoping being around mine will help Mark. It's becoming more obvious each day that my son needs more than I can give him, especially after last night at the church."

"You don't have just your family to help you. I'm here, too. We'll find an answer to what's going on with Mark. How was he after he got home last night?"

"He didn't say much on the drive home or later. He went to his room and played his CDs — loudly."

"You said he's still asleep. When did he go to sleep?"

"Not until after four this morning."

A frown creased his forehead and slashed his mouth. "When did this sleeplessness begin?"

"Six, seven, maybe eight months ago. It happened gradually. He would stay up later and later. By the end of school this year it was severely affecting his grades. He has always been a good student up until this year. He made several Ds and the rest were Cs. Do you think he's suffering from depression?"

"That's a possibility. Hopefully I can spend some time with him, maybe convince him to come in for some tests. Did he say anything about coming to the youth group on Sunday night?"

"He didn't say no, which is a good thing. At least he's thinking about it." The oven timer went off and Kathleen removed the last loaf of bread. The aroma filled the kitchen with warmth and cozy thoughts.

"Good. Getting him involved with people might help him."

Sitting back down at the table, Kathleen sipped at her now-cold tea. "Maybe. In the past few years my life has certainly changed. If you'd asked me two years ago what I was going to be doing now, I wouldn't have thought this."

"Unexpected things happen in life." He sighed, running his finger along the rim of the glass. "I don't let it worry me too much. My life is in God's hands."

Kathleen curled her fingers tighter around her empty mug and carefully placed it on the table. She used to think that until she'd lost John. "Have you ever wondered why bad things happen to good people?"

"Like your husband dying?"

"Yes." Her chest tightened, trapping her breath.

"God has a plan for us. We don't always know what it is. If we put our trust in Him, He will show us."

Kathleen stared down at her mug. "When John first died, I couldn't bring myself to pray or go to church. I only started attending again recently." She brought her gaze to Jared's, his image blurry. "John was such a good man. I still don't understand why he had to die so young. A freak accident took him away just like that." She snapped her fingers.

"Maybe John fulfilled what God had planned for him. He's now with our Lord in heaven. That's not a bad thing."

"It was for me."

"But you're only one of God's children. He's concerned for all of His children."

Kathleen wasn't sure if she could accept Jared's words. His strong faith obviously helped him overcome a lot of difficult problems, such as the death of his wife, but their situations were not the same.

Jared started to say something when the ring of his cell phone cut him off. "Just a minute." He retrieved the instrument from the pocket of his shorts and flipped it on. "Dr. Matthews here."

As he listened to the other person on the phone, the lines in his forehead returned. A frown darkened his eyes and his grip tightened until his knuckles whitened. "I'll come home immediately."

When he disconnected, Kathleen asked, "Is something wrong at home?"

"Hannah. She's locked herself in the bathroom and won't come out."

"Why?"

"I'm not sure, but from what the housekeeper said, I think my daughter has started her period."

"Oh, I see."

His gaze embraced hers. "You probably do see, even better than me. Hannah doesn't respond to our housekeeper that much. She calls her the old battle-ax. I'm not sure my daughter will want to talk to me about this, and I know she won't with Mrs. Davis." He attempted a grin that failed. "That's why she's in the bathroom right now with the door locked. She refuses to talk to the housekeeper."

"Do you think she would talk to me?"

"I don't know. But I'm willing to try if you are." This time his grin stayed in place. "I'm a desperate dad."

"Well, in that case, let me come with you and give it a try. It can be a confusing time for a girl. Have you talked to her about her body changing? Did your wife?"

"No, Alice didn't. I tried and Hannah wouldn't listen. I gave her a book about it."

"Did she read it?"

"I think so. But then, knowing Hannah, she may have flipped through it just to please me. She's one girl who I don't think is too pleased to go into womanhood. She's still quite a tomboy. She can get dirtier than Terry when she's playing."

Kathleen rose. "It's not an easy time."

"For the dad or the daughter?"

"Both. You're a doctor. You're very

knowledgeable about all the changes that Hannah will go through. This is just the beginning."

Jared reached for his plate and glass and took them to the sink. "Why do you think I'm so desperate? I feel ill-equipped to handle this."

"I know what you mean. There have been issues with my son that I felt so awkward talking to him about. But I believe young people should be kept informed, and I want to be the one informing, not some friend who may or may not have the facts right."

Outside on the porch Jared descended the steps. "When I signed up to be a parent, I didn't realize all that it entailed."

"Parents rarely do the first time around."

"How about the first time with each sex? Raising a boy is so different from raising a girl."

"You won't get an argument from me."

"You see, I knew there was something about you I liked. No arguments."

She laughed. "Don't count on it. I love to argue when I feel I'm right."

"Is that a warning?"

"You bet." Kathleen lifted her face to the sun and relished the warmth on her skin. The June air was still cool, the breeze caressing. She inhaled then exhaled a deep breath, wishing the beauty of the day could wash away the turmoil churning in her stomach. "Before long summer will be in full swing, searing heat and all." She peered toward the Ozark Mountains. "But for right now there's still a touch of spring in this corner of Arkansas."

"My favorite time of year." Jared started down the sidewalk toward the corner.

"When everything is reborn," she said, falling into step beside him.

Ten minutes later Jared turned up the walk to a two-story redbrick house with two massive oak trees in front. Kathleen paused to admire the landscape. The yard was mowed and neatly trimmed with well-tended orange and yellow marigolds by the porch.

She whistled. "What a beautiful yard. You and my dad have a lot in common. I think you'll be a great candidate to take care of the gardens at church."

"The housekeeper takes care of the inside. I take care of the outside. I enjoy getting out and puttering around in the yard. Makes me forget about my worries for a short period of time."

"You see, that's how I feel about the kitchen."

"How does Mark feel about yard work?"

"He used to love it. He and John would spend hours working outside. Now he doesn't want to do anything. I feel like a nag just getting him to mow our lawn."

She followed Jared up the steps to a huge porch that ran the length of his house. A profusion of potted plants adorned it as well as a swing and natural wicker furniture with bright yellow cushions. "Do you spend a lot of time out here?"

"When I can, especially in the early morning and the evening right before the sun sets."

"Nice times of the day."

"It's my quiet time." Again his grin appeared, dimpling his cheeks. "At least the morning is my quiet time. The kids aren't up yet. I can't really say that about the evening. I've helped with many a homework assignments on that swing."

The front door swung open and Terry hurried outside. "Dad, Hannah won't let anyone in. Let's call the fire department. They can rescue her."

Jared put his hand on his son's shoulder to stop his forward momentum. "I think they have better things to do with their time than that."

"Then how are we gonna get her out?"

"She's not stuck in there. She can come

out anytime she wants."

"Mrs. Davis has tried everything. She yelled at her. She tried to bribe her. Nothing's worked."

"Let's go see what we can do." Jared hugged his son to his side for a few seconds before entering the house.

Upstairs Mrs. Davis, who had brown hair streaked with gray and pulled back into a severe bun, stood in the middle of the hallway in front of what was obviously the main bathroom, tapping her foot against the brown-carpeted floor. Her irritated expression underscored her exasperated stance.

"I'll take over, Mrs. Davis. Thanks for letting me know."

The rotund, large woman huffed and rushed past Jared, Terry and Kathleen, mumbling about being behind in her work.

Jared approached the closed door and leaned against it. "Hannah, come out and let's talk."

"No! Go away. I hate being a girl."

"I can't do that, Hannah," Jared said in a gentle voice. "Kathleen has come over to see you."

Kathleen stepped closer until she, too, was leaning into the door. "I thought maybe you and I could talk woman-to-woman."

Nothing came from Hannah for almost three minutes, then Kathleen heard the lock click and the door eased open.

"Come in."

Kathleen went into the bathroom. Terry tried to follow. His sister blocked his way with her hands on her hips. She stuck out her lower lip, her eyes pinpoints, silently daring him to enter her domain.

"Terry, please go help Mrs. Davis now," Jared said behind the boy.

Terry groaned but headed down the hall. Hannah immediately locked the door again. Kathleen sat on the lip of the bathtub while the twelve-year-old plopped down on the closed lid of the toilet. Her hands folded in front of her, the young girl stared at the cream-colored tile on the floor.

Kathleen waited a few minutes to see if Hannah would say anything. When she didn't speak, Kathleen said, "I can still remember my first time. I was scared. I didn't know what to feel. My mother is great, but she was always uncomfortable talking about things like that. I wasn't sure what was happening to me."

Hannah looked straight at her. "Dad gave me a book. It explained everything. That's not the problem."

When the young girl didn't elaborate,

Kathleen asked, "What *is* the problem? Maybe I can help."

Hannah's bottom lip quivered. "Can you stop it?"

"No, it's a natural routine in a woman's life."

"But I don't want it. I don't feel well. I —"

Kathleen squatted in front of Hannah. "Do you have cramps?"

She shook her head. "I'm not myself. I don't know how to describe it."

Kathleen placed her hand over the young girl's. "Out of sorts?"

"Yes."

"That's common. Our body's hormones can affect our moods."

Her eyes watery with unshed tears, Hannah bit her teeth into her bottom lip. "Why does this have to happen to me?"

Kathleen hid her smile, wondering how many women have thought that very same question. "It's part of God's plan. As you know from the book you read, having periods is tied to a woman being able to have children."

"I don't wanna change. I like everything the way it is," Hannah said with a sniff.

"That, too, is part of life. Change will happen. I guarantee it." Kathleen remembered her earlier comments about her life changing. She hadn't wished hers to change, either.

"Can I still play sports when I'm — ?" Hannah's question faded into silence, her teeth digging into her lower lip even more.

"Of course. But as you become a young woman, you'll need to see about getting things like a bra. Do you have one now?"

Hannah's eyes grew round. "No! I don't want one."

"When you play sports, it's better to wear one. I could go with you to get a sports bra if you want."

"Sports bra?" Hannah thought that over for a moment. "Okay — I guess so. If I have to."

"Can I help you with anything else? Do you know how to take care of yourself? Do you have everything you need?"

"Yes. Dad gave me a box of pads when he gave me the book to read."

"Do you have any other concerns I can help you with?" Kathleen pushed to her feet, suddenly realizing she missed not having a daughter. John and she had wanted more children, but it wasn't to be.

"When can we go shopping?"

Noticing the puffy redness around Hannah's eyes, Kathleen took the washcloth from the towel rack and wet it.

After handing it to the young girl, she said, "I'll talk to your father and set a date if that's okay with you."

Hannah wiped her face, mumbling into the terry cloth, "You don't think Dad will get mad if I go with you instead of him?"

Kathleen smiled at the young girl. "I think he'll be all right with just the two of us going."

"Thanks, Kathleen," Hannah said as Kathleen left the bathroom.

Jared leaned against the wall across from her. When he saw her, he shoved away and started toward the bathroom, worry creasing his brow, his eyes dark. "Do I need to talk to Hannah?"

Kathleen stopped him with a hand on his arm. The second her skin touched his she knew her mistake. Her fingertips tingled as though an electrical current had passed between them. She immediately dropped her hand to her side. "She's fine. Give her a few minutes to wash her face, compose herself."

He stared at the closed door, the hard line of his jaw attesting to his continued concern. "Are you sure she —"

The door opened and Hannah emerged, her face scrubbed clean, all evidence of her tears gone. "Dad, I'm sorry." Her gaze remained glued to the floor, her shoulders hunched. "I didn't mean for you to come home."

His tension siphoned from his expression, the taut muscles in his neck and shoulders relaxing as a grin appeared on his face. "I'm just glad you're okay. You know you can talk to me about anything."

A blush tinted Hannah's cheeks. She shuffled from one foot to the other.

"Well, I guess just about anything. I know there'll be some things that will be hard for you to talk to me about. But I want you to realize that I'll love you no matter what."

Hannah finally glanced up, tears misting her eyes. "I know, Daddy. I love you." She threw herself into his arms and hugged him tightly.

When Jared stepped back, his arms stayed on Hannah's shoulders, compelling her to continue looking at him. "There isn't anything I wouldn't do for you." He cleared his throat. "Now how about a glass of lemonade? We could drink it on the porch."

"I'm supposed to meet Bobby and the gang at his house. I'd better go before they start asking questions. You and Kathleen have a glass of lemonade. She has something to ask you." Hannah flew down the stairs, leaving her astonished father watching her.

"You're wonderful with your daughter."

Jared swung his attention to Kathleen. "What do you need to ask me?"

"I promised I would take Hannah shopping — for a bra."

"Oh, I didn't — I should have realized."

"Most fathers don't want even to acknowledge that their little girl is growing up. It doesn't surprise me you didn't think about it."

He plowed his hand through his hair. "What else have I forgotten?"

"You're doing fine. Being a single parent isn't easy. I never realized how much I depended on John until he was gone."

A frown descended on Jared's face. He started for the stairs. "Do you want a glass of lemonade?"

The rigid set to his shoulders spoke more than words. There was a lot of pain bottled up in Jared. She wasn't even sure he was aware of how much. Having gone through her own kind of pain, she wished she could wipe his away with the brush of her hand. Maybe being there as a friend would help not only Hannah but him, as well. She liked being needed as a woman to a man and missed that since John's death.

"That sounds refreshing after our near jog here."

"I'm sorry about that. I've always walked fast and with the problem concerning Hannah —" He shrugged, not finishing his sentence.

"I understand. I'm just glad I could help."

"Make yourself comfortable on the porch. I'll get the lemonades and bring them out."

Kathleen made her way to the porch and sat in the wooden swing. She couldn't forget the swift change in Jared's demeanor. The dark shadows in his eyes revealed his struggle to maintain his composure, to push memories away. How much was he keeping inside? Men often didn't talk about their emotions. They locked them away, denying they existed. Her yearning to feel needed, to help, grew.

The bang of the screen door alerted her to his approach. She glanced up and saw that he had himself under control, a neutral expression on his face. He handed her one glass and folded himself into a wicker chair opposite the swing. For just a second regret whipped through her — she told herself it was only because it was harder to carry on a conversation with him several yards away instead of next to her on the swing.

He took a sip of his drink. "Did Mark say

anything more about why he smashed his guitar?"

She stiffened, reminded of her own set of problems. "No, he just insisted that he didn't want to play it anymore." Kathleen drank some of her lemonade to quench the ache in her throat.

"In my practice I've seen some teenagers have a rougher time growing up than others. Keep watching him closely. Be there for him when he needs you."

"That's just it. He doesn't need me. He spends most of his time alone in his room when he's at home."

"Maybe he was more upset about the move than you thought."

"When we got home last night, I talked to him again about it and he told me he didn't care." Guilt at the inability to help her son cloaked her in a heavy blanket, pressing her down.

"Did you believe him?"

"Yes. The last couple of months in Shreveport he wasn't hanging around his friends like he used to. I tried talking to him about it but didn't get anywhere. Do you think I was just hoping he didn't care because I wanted to move?" She needed someone to tell her she had made the right decision in coming home.

49

Jared put his half-empty glass on the wicker table next to him. "Why did you want to move back to Crystal Springs?"

"I needed a change. My memories of Crystal Springs have always been fond ones."

"But not Shreveport?"

She downed the rest of her lemonade as though she hadn't drunk anything in days. "In Shreveport I found myself unable to move on in my life. I tried for a year and a half and finally acknowledged it wasn't going to happen if I stayed." Everywhere I turned I was reminded of how little control I have over my life, she silently added. I need control back.

"When you move, the memories go with you."

"You can't hide from yourself?"

"Exactly." He leaned forward resting his elbows on his knees and clasping his hands, nothing casual about him. "Don't give up on God. He hasn't abandoned you."

"I've lost my husband and now I feel like I'm losing my son."

"If I can do anything about it, I won't let you lose your son."

The vehemence in his voice underscored his intentions, making Kathleen feel that she wasn't alone. If she wasn't careful, she could come to depend on Jared Matthews a great deal and she couldn't let that happen. John's death had rocked her world. She wouldn't go through that kind of pain ever again.

CHAPTER THREE

Returning to the church's recreational hall Sunday evening, Kathleen cracked the door open and peered inside. Twenty teenagers sat listening to Jared describe their latest fundraiser. Mark had reluctantly agreed to coming this evening and was next to his cousin, Shane, his gaze on the floor. She wasn't even sure if her son was hearing a word Jared was saying. Mark's features were devoid of any expression. Seeing her son like that sent a chill down her spine.

Kathleen slipped inside the room while Jared wrapped up what everyone needed to do before the next week's meeting. He caught her eye and smiled.

"Before we adjourn to the volleyball court, let's pray," Jared said, bowing his head. "Dear Heavenly Father, be with each and every one of these young people as they go through life. Help them to make the right choices and be there for them when they don't. Amen." Jared looked over the sea of teenagers. "The first game starts in ten minutes."

The recreational hall emptied, all except for Mark, Kathleen and Jared. Mark slouched in his chair, continuing to stare at the tiled floor.

"Are you going to join us, Mark?" Jared asked, weaving his way through the rows of chairs toward Kathleen.

Mark shot Kathleen a look that spoke of boredom and disinterest. "Yeah, I guess."

He pushed his lanky body, clad in black jeans and a black T-shirt, to his feet and trudged toward the door that led to outside.

When he disappeared from view, Kathleen released her pent-up breath in a rush. "I gather he wasn't an involved member of the group."

"No, but I did catch him listening a few times."

"I hope he'll get involved more. Otherwise this summer will be an extremely long one for him. I think all he'd do is sit in his room all day if I didn't make him do chores around the house or help his grandparents some."

"Besides listening to his music, what else does he do in his room?"

"He likes to draw. He's been drawing a lot in a sketch book I got for him."

"Have you looked at the sketches?"

"No, he won't show them to me, and I haven't wanted to invade his privacy."

"Sometimes parents have to do things they don't want to in order to protect their children."

"You think I should check the drawings out without him knowing?"

"They may tell you what's going on in his head. Try to get him to show you." Jared swept his arm across his body. "Now, come on out and join the festivities. Have you ever played volleyball?"

"Back in my younger days," Kathleen replied, her mind dwelling on what Jared had said about Mark's drawings. She had always respected her son's privacy before, but — The thought of what she must do made her shiver.

"It's time to renew your skills," Jared's words cut into her musing. "Everyone plays. We rotate teams."

Stepping outside, Kathleen surveyed the newly mowed yard at the side of the church, the scent of cut grass peppering the air. A volleyball court with a net was set up near the picnic tables located under four large maple trees. "Which unlucky team gets me?"

"Now where's your positive thinking?"

"When I heard you mention volleyball, I

think I left it back in the recreational hall. I'm not very athletic."

"That's fine." He smiled, his blue eyes glittering. "I'll just make sure I'm on the opposing team."

Kathleen sat on a bench next to Jared and watched the first two teams play a game, her son, who used to be a good athlete, doing as little as possible. Again she wondered if she'd been wrong to come back to Crystal Springs. Maybe Mark needed familiar surroundings at this stage in his life. This town wasn't an unknown to her son, but it wasn't the place where he'd grown up. Self-doubts plagued her. She didn't know what to do anymore. In the past she'd always had John to talk things over with and to support any decision she'd made.

"This is for fun," Jared whispered, his arm brushing against hers.

The brief touch drew her attention. Tiny sparks of awareness feathered outward. "I know."

"I wasn't sure. Your look of intense concentration tells me otherwise."

She relaxed the knotted tension that held her stiff and uncurled her fingers. Her nails had left an indentation in her palms. She hadn't even realized how tense she'd been until Jared had said something. "I'm not the most graceful person when it comes to playing a sport. I was always the last one picked for a team. My reputation preceded me."

"We don't pick teams. You'll be filling in for Anne, who is sick. Your team is up next."

Kathleen examined the clear blue sky. "Too bad. There isn't a raincloud anywhere to be seen."

"Nope. You're stuck." He took her hand within his. "I know you're worried about Mark. I'll help you figure out what's wrong. I promise."

His sweet words, full of confidence, produced a lump in her throat. Jared would discover what was going on with her son. That thought brought tears of relief to her eyes. She blinked, a tear coursing down her face. Jared didn't say anything, but he brushed his thumb across her cheek, the rough texture of his finger in sharp contrast to his soft touch. He then squeezed her hand gently, silently conveying his support as they both twisted about to stare at the teenagers battling on the volleyball court.

Five minutes later the game ended with Mark's team winning. Her son gave his cousin a high five, but the elation she usually saw in Mark's expression when he won wasn't visible.

Jared stood and extended his hand to Kathleen. "It's show time. Ready?"

"No, will that make a difference?"

"No."

"That's what I thought. I'll be a sub."

Laughter shone in his eyes. "There are no subs. Everyone gets to play. That's the beauty of this setup."

"That's your opinion, not mine. I definitely think that's a major flaw. What if someone gets hurt?"

"We remove a player from the other side and play on."

"Do you remove the injured player before you resume playing or do you just play around him?"

His laughter spiced the air, much like the aroma of baking bread, warm with cozy thoughts brought to mind. "You'll be all right. Remember, I'm a doctor."

"Now that's really reassuring."

"You might want to stretch some before the game." Jared bent over and touched the ground, then did several lunges.

Having been a runner in high school, Kathleen knew the importance of stretching her muscles before a workout. And she was afraid the next half hour or so would definitely be a workout. She ran through a stretching routine, hoping she didn't make a fool of herself.

She was thankful that she was placed on the back row as far away from the net and spiked balls as possible. On television she'd seen the killer volleyball matches at the Summer Olympic Games. She didn't want a ball stuffed down her throat.

For the first two serves she only had to shift from foot to foot and pretend she was alert and ready. When the ball slammed across the net for the third time, it came right at her. She had to do something — fast. Miscalculating where it was going to land, she dove the last foot to punch the ball into the air. It shot out of bounds. The other team cheered, Jared the loudest.

By the time she rotated to the front of the line, she faced Jared with only the netting between them. His smile was full of mischief, and she had a funny feeling it would be all directed at her. He leaped into the air and smacked the ball toward her. She positioned herself to return it.

Before she had a chance to connect with the fast-approaching ball, someone knocked into her, yelling in her ear, "I've got it."

She smashed into the ground, her left shoulder cushioning her fall. She blew out gritty sand that made up the court and pushed her hair out of her face. Her left cheek burned where it had struck the sand-covered earth.

A loud roar of triumph filled the air while she brushed bits of grit from her eyes. Through the blur she saw Jared coming toward her, concern on his face. He knelt down.

"Are you all right, Kathleen? Are you hurt anywhere?"

"Does all over count as one place or many?"

He ran his hands up her left arm and over her shoulder. She winced.

"It doesn't feel like it's broken, but to be on the safe side I think you should let me take you to the hospital and get an X ray."

"I don't want to go to the hospital." Suddenly Kathleen felt many eyes on her. She scanned the young people standing around her and Jared. "What happened?"

"I'm sorry, Mrs. Somers. I thought you weren't gonna get the ball so I wanted to help. I misjudged."

"But I was right there." Using her arms to try and push herself to her feet, she attempted to stand. The pain in her shoulder intensified, and she fell back, sucking in a deep breath.

The young boy dropped his head. "Yeah,

but you were there that last time, too, and missed."

"That's okay, Aaron."

"Can I help you to your feet, ma'am?"

"No," she said so quickly the teenager blinked. "I mean, Jared is going to take me to the hospital. I'm sure I'm fine. It's just a precaution." Through the crowd now surrounding her, she saw her son, hanging back but watching her. "You could give Mark a ride home, Aaron."

"Sure, I can do that. Are you sure I can't help you?"

"Yes, I'm sure." The pain in her shoulder eased its intensity. With her right arm she maneuvered herself to her knees.

Jared supported her around the waist. "Take it easy."

As the teenagers began to scatter, she said, "Oh, I plan on taking it slow and easy."

"I had no idea you'd go to such lengths to get out of playing volleyball."

The teasing light in Jared's eyes made her laugh. "I told you I don't do sports." She observed the quickly disappearing crowd of teens. "As soon as Aaron's been gone five minutes, I'm driving home. I have no intentions of going to the hospital. I'm fine." She tried to move her shoulder and groaned.

"I can see that."

Jared moved so close she wondered if he could hear her heart pounding. "Some rest, ice, and I'll be good as new."

"Appease this doctor and let me take you to check your shoulder out."

"But what about my car?"

"You can get it tomorrow. I'll even come by and give you a ride to the church to get it. I won't sleep well tonight knowing you may be in pain because I persuaded you to play volleyball."

His touch on her arm drew her gaze upward to his face. The plea in his eyes and the ache in her shoulder finally caused her to nod.

"See, I told you there wasn't anything to worry about. I'll be as good as new in a few days." Kathleen rolled her shoulder to prove her point. A stab of pain shot down her arm, and she winced. "Okay, maybe it will be a little longer than that."

Jared pulled into her driveway and switched off the engine. "Still, I'm glad you got it X rayed. I feel better knowing for sure and the medication should help you."

"Do you want to come in for a cup of coffee? Decaf or I'd be up all night."

"Sure. Mrs. Davis doesn't turn into a pumpkin until at least nine o'clock."

Kathleen slid from the car, trying to hold her upper body still as she moved. "How hard was it to find Mrs. Davis?"

"Hard. A good housekeeper is not easy to come by. She isn't too bad. My children are safe with her, and she performs her job efficiently."

"But?"

"But she isn't the warmest person around. And right now Hannah needs a womanly touch, which she isn't going to get with Mrs. Davis."

Kathleen inserted her key into the lock and opened her door. "What about your mother-in-law?"

His expression tensed into a frown. "Not much help there. She doesn't have much to do with Terry and Hannah. We see her for special occasions like birthdays and the holidays."

"I'm sorry to hear that." She placed her purse on the table in the entry hall. "Come on into the kitchen while I put the coffee on." As she scooped the coffee into the filter, she continued, "I can help, especially with Hannah."

He offered her a smile that eased the tension from him. "Thanks. I may take you up on that."

"Don't forget I promised Hannah I would

take her shopping. I was thinking some time this week."

"Fine. Whatever fits into your schedule. Hannah has talked about it, and I think she's actually excited, which is a first since I usually have to drag her kicking and screaming to shop for clothes."

"That'll change as she grows older."

"There's a part of me that will be thrilled to see my daughter grow out of being a tomboy."

"But there's a part that won't be happy?"

"Sure. The part that is dreading her first date."

"You aren't the only father who feels that way. It's a constant battle to be one step ahead of our kids." The coffee dripping into the glass pot was the only sound Kathleen heard. She cocked her head and listened for a moment. No music coming from her son's room. In fact, the house was awfully silent. "Which reminds me, I want to make sure Mark got home okay. I'll be right back."

"Aaron's not a bad driver, better than he is a volleyball player."

"I'm sure he is. But I usually hear Mark moving around. His room is right above the kitchen. It's too quiet for my peace of mind."

Kathleen headed upstairs, her heart beginning to beat a shade faster. Something wasn't right. She knocked on Mark's door and waited a minute. Nothing. Pushing it open, she saw chaos all about her. Clothes were thrown everywhere. Drawers were left open. The bed was stripped of its linens and they lay on the floor beside it as though her son now slept on the carpet. She moved into the middle of the room, shaking her head. A year ago her son wouldn't have had any of his belongings out of place. Like everything else in his life, that had changed, too.

Kathleen started to leave but caught a glimpse of his drawing pad, hidden under a pile of dirty clothes. Chewing on her bottom lip, she reached for the paper, hesitated, then snatched it up. Quickly before she changed her mind, she flipped through the pictures, afraid to look at what her son was drawing, and yet compelled to check this aspect of his life out. Maybe there were answers in his drawings that would help her.

The first drawing was of their old house. Another was of his guitar. Picture after picture seemed perfectly normal with nothing unusual portrayed. Relief shimmered through her, and she returned the pad to its hiding place.

When Kathleen left the bedroom, any relief she felt evaporated as she made her way down the stairs. Where was Mark? It was only eight o'clock and he was sixteen, but still she couldn't help the worry that swelled inside her, especially after his erratic behavior two nights ago.

She hurried into the kitchen and went straight to the phone, punching in her sister's number. "Is Mark over there?" She couldn't keep the urgency from her voice.

"No. Shane came home a few minutes ago and went to his room. Do you want me to ask him if he knows where Mark is?"

Kathleen's grip on the receiver tightened until pain radiated down her arm. "Please." When she heard Laura put the phone down, Kathleen glanced toward Jared.

"What's wrong?"

"Mark wasn't in his room. No note on the table in the entry hall telling me where he is. He knows he's supposed to let me know where he's going if I'm not here when he leaves." Panic nibbled at the edges of her composure as all kinds of thoughts — none good — swirled in her mind. Again, as so many times of late, she felt her life spinning out of control. Her life felt much like the chaos in her son's room.

"Kathleen, Shane doesn't know where he is. Aaron dropped him off at your house forty minutes ago. Do you want me to come over and help you look for him?"

"No, I'm sure he's fine," Kathleen answered, wishing her declaration was true. But with Mark she wasn't sure anymore. She could still vividly remember the time in Shreveport when he had run away instead of going to the doctor. "Thanks, Laura." The clamoring of her heart thundered in her ears as she replaced the receiver in its cradle. Her hands shook, and she clasped them together to keep them from trembling.

"Maybe he's here somewhere or outside."

"I shouldn't have gone to the hospital. I should have come home, then this wouldn't be happening."

Jared stepped in front of Kathleen and commanded her full attention by grasping her upper arms, his nearness forcing her to look into his eyes. "Let's check the whole house first, then outside."

The sound of the front door slamming shut startled Kathleen. She jerked away from Jared and headed toward the entry hall. Mark was halfway up the stairs.

"Where have you been?" She grimaced at the harsh tone in her voice. She needed to remain calm. Nothing good came from confronting her son. It only made the situation worse lately.

He slowly peered over his shoulder. A

long moment passed with nothing said, then he shrugged and mumbled, "Out. Walking."

Kathleen forced herself to take a deep, calming breath, but still her stomach muscles remained clenched in a tight knot. "You're supposed to write me a note telling me where you're going."

He lifted his shoulders in another shrug. "Forgot." He resumed his progress up the stairs.

Kathleen counted to ten, then twenty, but nothing soothed her shredded nerves. She couldn't shake the feeling something was terribly wrong. Watching her son disappear down the hall, she sensed Jared standing behind her. She whirled. "I'm beginning to wonder if he can put a sentence of more than a word or two together anymore." She tried to smile, but it wavered about the corners of her mouth and vanished almost immediately.

"I've thought that many times while having a conversation with my children. I know they can because I've heard them with their friends. But sometimes talking to them is like pulling teeth."

"At least he's home and I don't have to go out searching for him. I used not to have to worry like this, but lately, especially since the talent show, I don't know what to think when it comes to Mark."

Jared took a deep breath. "I think the coffee is ready. Why don't we sit and talk over a cup?"

The aroma of coffee teased her senses. The idea of sharing a quiet, adult conversation with Jared roused her interest. "That sounds great. I can bring our coffee into the living room if you want."

"Let's drink it in the kitchen. I always think of that room as the heart of a house."

With one last glance toward the top of the stairs, Kathleen led the way. "I like that. I probably spend more time in here than any room if I don't count the hours I sleep."

"When I was growing up, that was an important part of the house. Now I hardly set foot in my kitchen. Mrs. Davis prefers us staying out when she is creating her meals. At least she's a good cook. I wish Hannah could learn to cook."

"I could show her some dishes if she wants to learn."

Jared grinned, deep lines fanning out from the corners of his eyes, indicating the man was used to smiling a lot. "I don't think she has thought much about it. I just think it's something she should know."

"But not Terry?"

"Actually I think he should learn, too, but I don't see Mrs. Davis being their teacher."

But Jared saw Kathleen teaching them. He should back off from her right now, but he couldn't. Hannah needed someone like Kathleen in her life — even if it was only as a friend. He couldn't deny his child that. He would just have to be extra careful to protect his own heart.

"When I take Hannah shopping, I'll see if she would like to have some lessons."

"Maybe I could meet you two for lunch."

"Hannah would love that. I thought Thursday would be a good day to go." Kathleen removed two mugs from the cabinet and poured coffee into each.

"Are you two going to the mall?"

Kathleen nodded, handing Jared his mug.

"Then I'll meet you at the south entrance at noon and we can go to lunch." Taking a seat at the glass table, Jared settled back and scanned the room. "I like this. Warm. Inviting."

"It was the first room I put together. I like to cook and it was so hard digging around in boxes trying to find what I needed." Kathleen did her own survey of the kitchen, relaxing the tension that had gripped her ever since she had discovered Mark gone. The forest greens and deep reds of the plaid wallpaper added a richness to the walnut-finished cabinets. The light brown tiles that covered the floor lent a cool refreshing feel to the room. "I think this was what sold me on the house. It's large and open with plenty of windows to let in the sunshine."

Jared sipped his coffee, his gaze locking with hers over the mug's rim. "I can't believe you got your house in order in two weeks. I can still remember when we moved to Crystal Springs. It took us months to feel at home in our house."

"I can be a very determined lady when I set my mind to a job. I need order in my surroundings. I'm much happier that way and learned long ago it was easier on me to keep things in their place."

Her words brought back a memory that lambasted Jared. He put down his mug with more force than he intended, its sound against the glass piercing the quiet.

"What's wrong?"

Jared closed his eyes for a few seconds, the memory still ingrained in his mind. When he looked at Kathleen, he saw the worry etched into her features. "I just thought of something that happened once, that's all."

Kathleen didn't say anything, and her silence prodded him to fill the void. For some reason it felt right to talk to her even though he hadn't discussed Alice's problem in a long time, hadn't wanted to rehash something he'd rather forget.

"My wife hated housework, so one weekend I decided to help her. We had only been married a few years. That weekend I discovered one liquor bottle stashed behind the cleaning supplies under the sink and another one on the top shelf of the linen closet." He paused, still sharply remembering the cold feel of the bottle in his hands as he had shown it to her. "I hadn't realize Alice even drank. She knew how I felt about it."

"So she kept it hidden from you?"

"Not after I confronted her with the two bottles. From then on she was open about her drinking." Memories of watching his wife empty a bottle into a large glass then down it shuddered through him.

"That had to be hard."

"Yes." Jared took another sip of his coffee, cupping the mug to mask the quivering in his hands. "I've seen what alcohol can do to a person, medically speaking. In some ways I wished I had remained ignorant of her problem."

"Ignorance is bliss?"

He placed his mug on the mat, this time

being careful and said in a tightly controlled voice, "She wouldn't let me help her. There were times my frustration level was unbearable. It's hard watching someone self-destruct."

Kathleen slid her hand across the cool glass and covered his. "How did you handle the stress?"

"I worked harder and longer at building my practice. By that time we had moved to Crystal Springs. And when I wasn't working, I threw myself into the activities at the church we attended. If I hadn't, I don't know how I would have made it, especially when Alice became pregnant with Terry unexpectedly. I didn't want any more children. I had seen the effects of alcohol on unborn babies."

Kathleen squeezed his hand, her heart swelling. "Terry seems fine."

"He is." Jared blew out a long breath. "Thankfully Alice agreed to go into rehab while she was pregnant. Everything seemed fine for a while, but a few months after Terry was born, she started drinking again and was killed in a drunk driving accident."

Tears stung Kathleen's eyes, a lump lodged in her throat. "I'm sorry."

Jared blinked, slipping his hand from hers. He straightened, a flush to his face. "I

72

didn't mean to tell you that. It's not something I like to relive."

"Maybe you should. It's important to work through our feelings in order to get beyond them."

"That life *is* behind me."

The look of doubt in his eyes belied the force of his words. "Is it?"

He held her gaze for a few seconds, then glanced away. "Yes. Living through it once was enough." He rose in one fluid motion. "I'd better be going. Tomorrow will be a long day."

Kathleen walked Jared to the door and watched him descend the steps out front. The droop to his shoulders attested to his weariness. The tight grin he gave her as he waved good-bye emphasized he wasn't over what he had gone through with his wife. He might think it was behind him, but Kathleen knew it wasn't.

Chapter Four

"Can I see what you have in that package?" Jared asked as Hannah and Kathleen approached him in the mall.

His daughter's eyes grew round. She quickly hid the bag behind her back. "No."

Jared took in her rosy cheeks and knew he had stepped into territory best left to the women. "Did you spend all my money?" That wasn't a safe question for a man to ask, either, he realized after he'd said it.

"Not yet," Kathleen said with a laugh. "But if you like what Hannah wants to buy, yes."

"You want my opinion?"

"Since you're paying, Kathleen thought so."

"Let's eat first, then I'll take a look at it. Where do you want to have lunch?"

"The Greasy Spoon," Hannah said, her face lit with a huge grin.

"What's that?" asked Kathleen. "I thought I knew most of the restaurants in Crystal Springs. Of course, I'm not sure any place called the Greasy Spoon should be considered a restaurant."

"It's fairly new," Jared answered, starting to walk. "It's at the other end of the mall. Not bad, if you like fried food. Hence the name *Greasy*."

Kathleen fell into step next to Jared with Hannah on her other side. As they made their way to the restaurant, Hannah veered off to the left, pulling her father over to the display window of the toy store.

She tapped the glass near an electronic game station, saying, "I want that for my birthday."

"That's not for another six months."

"Oh, yeah." Hannah's shoulders sagged. "You know it might be something you could get both Terry and I for the summer when it's too hot to play outside."

Jared pressed his lips together, his eyes dancing with merriment. "You've never had trouble finding something to do during the summer before. Why should this summer be any different?"

Hannah opened her mouth to say something, but instead snapped it closed, her expression screwing up into a thoughtful look.

"You could always save your allowance and buy it for yourself."

The girl brightened for a moment, but the

eagerness evaporated when she saw the price. "That'll take at least six months."

Jared placed his hand on Hannah's shoulder and began walking toward the other end of the mall. "Think how much it will mean to you when you finally get it. You could always earn some money. I weeded gardens for my neighbors at your age, which is where I learned to love yard work. I would dust for the Lunds. I walked Mrs. Wilson's dog for her because she couldn't. Now that, I loved doing."

"I could do that. I know Mr. Batchlear can't take his dog to the park like he used to. Maybe he would pay me to. And I bet I could get someone to let me weed their garden."

"Actually you could do mine if you want," Kathleen interjected.

"I can! Great. My first job!" Hannah jumped up and down, her blue eyes sparkling, her ponytail swinging from side to side in her excitement.

At the Greasy Spoon Hannah ran ahead to get a booth in the corner. Jared made his way at a much more subdued pace.

"I'm sorry, Jared. I should have asked you about that first."

Jared shook his head. "No, I think it's a great idea. It'll give her a goal to work

76

toward. I appreciate the offer."

The grin he sent Kathleen made her heart flip over. She swallowed hard and returned his smile. "And I'll have someone to weed the beds out front. Usually Mark does it, but he hasn't shown any interest this summer, and I hate yard work, so this is a win/win solution."

"Since your problem is solved," Jared slid into the booth across from Hannah, "maybe you could help me out with a problem."

"What?" Kathleen sat next to Hannah.

"I need another chaperone for the hiking trip this Saturday with the youth group. Phil has to work and can't make it. Are you game?"

"Hiking?"

"You said you like to do that with your family. Here's another opportunity to get Mark involved in the youth group and enjoy what I think will be a gorgeous day. The weatherman promises sunshine and mild temperatures."

"And you believe him?"

"Call me naive, but yes, I do."

Hannah giggled. "Dad always believes the man on the radio in the morning. Last week he took his umbrella to work and there wasn't a cloud in the sky all day."

"Mike Morgan goes to our church.

Someone has to support him."

"You're a friend no matter what." That was what Kathleen liked about Jared the most. She hadn't known him long, but she knew she could depend on him, and right now in her life that was important because of her son.

"I like to think so."

"Dad, wait till you see the outfit I picked out for church. Kathleen says I look good in it. It's a yellow-and-orange dress with no icky flowers on it."

"It's a dress? The last time you went shopping you told me you didn't want any dresses."

"Not for school, but I need one for church. The one I wear is too small. I'm growing up."

The look of surprise on Jared's face at Hannah's declaration brought a chuckle from Kathleen. She didn't think he was quite prepared for his daughter to turn into a young lady. Her transformation would prove to be interesting to watch. From their conversation today Kathleen didn't think Hannah was as much a tomboy as Jared thought.

"What else did you find?" Jared flipped open the menu.

Hannah blushed. "Just girl things." She

slipped from the booth, saying, "I'll be back in a sec," then headed for the restroom.

"A dress! I'm amazed you got her to agree even to try one on," Jared said, observing his daughter disappear into the ladies' room.

"We talked a little bit about how she would change over the next few years and what that meant. We got the sports bra and then a regular one. I stopped to admire some of the dresses and she gravitated toward the yellow-and-orange one. When I suggested she try it on, she did."

"How come it sounds so simple with you, but when I go shopping with her, it never is that simple?"

"You're a man."

"Thanks for noticing," he said with a wink and a grin.

Now it was Kathleen's turn to blush. She definitely had noticed. The heat flaming her cheeks went all the way down her neck. She could tell he took pride in keeping himself in good physical shape. With his dark hair and startling blue eyes, women must gravitate toward him. But the thing that made him the most appealing to her, and she suspected others, was his kindness and his caring attitude.

"You're easy to tease."

Kathleen pushed away her musings concerning Jared. She had no business thinking of him in any way other than a friend who wanted to help her son. "I told Hannah if she needed me to help her again that I would be happy to."

"You're a lifesaver. I'll encourage her to take you up on your offer."

"It lets you off the hook."

"You bet. I get tongue-tied just thinking about shopping with my daughter for more grown-up clothes. It was fine when she liked to dress as a boy, but realistically I know that will change, and I'm not sure how I feel about it. Next thing I know some young boy will be coming to the house to take her out on a date. That's gonna be mighty hard on me."

"It usually is for dads."

"But not moms?"

"We know what's going on in the daughter's head."

"Yeah, that's the problem. We know what's going on in the boy's head."

Kathleen laughed. "So it will be easier for you with Terry?"

"You bet. Guys don't wear makeup and lacy things."

"I meant what I said to Hannah. I'll help her whenever she needs it."

Jared's gaze shifted to his daughter returning from the restroom. "This dad will be in your debt."

As Hannah sat down beside her, Kathleen felt the rightness of the situation. She had enjoyed shopping with the young girl. For a few hours she had forgotten her problems with Mark. She had experienced what it would have been like if she'd had a daughter.

Jared made her feel important to his family, a good friend. She needed that in her time of trouble, to keep her focus on what was possible.

Kathleen stood on the edge of the hiking trail and scanned the valley below. Miles of green stretched before her. The tops of the trees gently swayed in the southerly breeze. The sun beat down upon her, chasing away the early-morning chill. When she lifted her gaze, she noticed not a cloud in the azure-blue sky. The scent of pine and earth filled her nostrils with each deep breath she took.

Even though behind her she heard the voices of the teenagers, she cleared her mind and allowed peace to settle over her. Closing her eyes, she imagined herself alone on this mountaintop with not a care in the world.

Someone jostled her. She glanced over her shoulder at a young man as he passed her on the path.

"Sorry, ma'am. Lost my footing."

"That's okay." She fell into step behind him, realizing her moment of daydreaming was over.

"I love hiking up here," Jared said, coming alongside her on the trail as it widened.

"Makes you feel on top of the world."

"Makes me feel closer to God. One of the best ways to celebrate His glory is to spend time in the outdoors admiring His work."

"I'm glad Hannah could come."

Jared leaned close to whisper, "She heard you were coming and her plans changed."

Jared's nearness shivered down her spine. His lime-scented aftershave lotion vied with the outdoorsy scents that enveloped her. "She did?"

"She asked to come along the second I got home that day you two went shopping. I'm surprised she didn't call me at the office. She was hopping around as though she could barely contain herself."

Pleased, Kathleen searched the path for the young girl and found her up ahead sandwiched between Shane and Mark. "I think I got more out of the shopping trip than she did. You've raised a wonderful daughter." Again the longing for a large family inundated Kathleen. John and she had tried to have more children, but it had never happened.

"You've made quite an impression on her. She's already canvassed the neighborhood for odd jobs and has gotten three of them besides yours. She's going to be busy for the next few weeks."

"Has she started baby-sitting yet?"

"I want her to take the Red Cross course first, then maybe she can sit during the daytime. She needs to be a little older for baby-sitting at night."

"I was thirteen. When's the course being taught?"

"In two weeks at the high school. Now she has Terry looking for ways to earn money. My neighbors don't know what hit them with both my children soliciting odd jobs."

"Maybe I can come up with something for Terry, too."

"I don't want you to go to any extra trouble. You've already done so much."

Kathleen came to a stop on the trail and faced him. Shielding her eyes from the sun, she looked at him. "What are friends for?

Helping each other is part of that. Your children are wonderful." And this feeling of helping him made their friendship feel more equal, as if she wasn't always depending on him. That was important to her.

A couple of the teenagers passed them on the path. Jared observed them walk ahead, then started forward, taking up the rear. "I think they are, but then I'm partial. I just want their lives to be as normal as possible. The last few years with Alice were very hard on the family." Tension took hold of his expression, firming his jawline, sharpening his eyes.

Every time he mentioned his deceased wife, Jared grew taut, stress swirling around him. Kathleen wasn't even sure he realized it. She suspected it was automatic with him. What little he had told her grieved her. Her marriage had been so different, a true partnership. "Children can often bounce back faster than adults."

"I'd have to agree with you on that. I don't know if I'll ever recover. Watching someone destroy herself and not being able to do anything about it was something I don't ever want to go through again."

Kathleen thought of Mark and his behavior lately. Maybe that was the real reason she'd returned home. She didn't know if she could deal with her son by herself anymore. It was times like this when she missed John the most, and yet the man beside her made her hope that there was a reason behind her son's changes and they would discover what it was.

The nearest teenager disappeared around a bend. Jared halted his progress and placed a hand on Kathleen's arm, stilling her movement. His warm touch comforted her, a connection to another who was rapidly becoming important to her.

"I'm glad you could talk Mark into coming today. It'll give me another chance to see how he behaves with the others." Jared slid his palm down her arm to grasp her hand. "On the ride in the van he was pretty quiet."

"I don't think he said one word." He linked their fingers together, and Kathleen felt the bond pierce defenses created after John's sudden death. That scared her. She needed those defenses. When she'd lost John, her life had fallen apart. That wasn't something she could go through again.

"But then with Shane and Connie monopolizing the whole conversation that would be hard. I don't think *I* said much." Jared held their clasped hands up between them, looking deep into her eyes.

Drawn to him, she leaned closer. Again his distinctive scent surrounded her. "I didn't notice. I was enjoying the beautiful scenery." Her words came out in a husky stream while a hollow feeling in the pit of her stomach expanded.

"Are you two coming?"

Shane's loud booming voice split the air and parted Kathleen and Jared. Standing on the trail up ahead were six teenagers all staring at them with broad smiles on their faces. Kathleen hurried forward, her cheeks flaming. She wished she could attribute it to the sun, but she couldn't, and the kids knew it. In the back of the group of six were Mark and Hannah. Hannah beamed; Mark scowled. He spun about and started along the trail with determination in every stride, his hands clenched at his sides. Hannah took the place next to Kathleen.

"Dad likes you," the young girl finally said.

"I like your father. He's a good friend." The words sounded empty even to her own ears, as though she wished there was much more to the relationship than friendship. She scoffed at that notion. Neither wanted anything but friendship.

"I'm gonna wear my new dress tomorrow to church. Candy says I don't know how to pick out pretty clothes. I'll show her."

"You'll knock their socks off with that dress."

"Maybe you could help me pick out another one for school."

Surprised at the request, Kathleen said, "Sure, when you get ready to go back in August, I can go with you if your dad says it's okay."

"He will. He likes you."

They were back to that again. Kathleen searched for something other than she and Jared to discuss.

"You're so much easier to talk to than Mrs. Davis," Hannah said before Kathleen could come up with another topic.

"How long has Mrs. Davis been your housekeeper?" Okay, this subject was a start in the right direction.

"Three years. Mom needed help, so Dad hired Mrs. Davis. She's okay. She cooks real good, but I bet you cook better. She won't let me help her in the kitchen."

"Next week I'm going to be making dozens of cookies for the church bake sale. Maybe you could help me."

Hannah stopped. "I can?"

"If it's okay with your —"

"Dad likes you. It'll be okay."

Kathleen clamped her lips together to

keep from moaning.

"When?"

"Tuesday afternoon."

"Can we make some peanut butter cookies? They're my favorite."

"Sure. I was going to bake several different kinds. Peanut butter will be one."

"And chocolate chip?"

Kathleen nodded, the young girl's eagerness catching.

"Sugar, too?"

"That sounds fine."

The rest of the hike up the trail to the lake nestled between two mountains was filled with Hannah talking about her favorite foods. By the time Kathleen reached their destination, her stomach rumbled with hunger, and she was ready to delve into the sacks and eat lunch an hour early. She leaned back against a tree trunk and surveyed the teenagers as they plopped their backpacks on the ground, then headed for the water.

"I almost came to rescue you."

Kathleen gasped, so intent on watching Mark standing off by himself that she hadn't heard Jared approach. "Rescue me?"

"From my daughter. When she gets going, she can talk a person's ear off."

"I have to admit I'm starved now. She

went from describing her favorite pizza to her favorite dessert. I think she likes ice cream and caramel about as much as I do. I could almost taste the hot caramel double dip sundae she told me was her favorite dessert. Where's the nearest store?"

His chuckle rippled down her length. "That's Hannah. I don't know how she keeps the weight off."

"Metabolism."

"That and the fact she can out-play most boys in soccer and baseball."

"She wants to help me bake cookies Tuesday. Is that all right?"

Jared's expression brightened, his eyes sparkling like the lake water with the sun glinting off its surface. "I don't want her to be a bother."

"She isn't. I asked her first. I could use the help since I'm going to make five or six dozen cookies."

"Do you need a tester? I'm quite good at that job." Jared's gaze roamed over the teenagers, some at the lake checking the temperature of the water, a few getting their fishing rods ready, others spreading their towels out to sunbathe.

"I bet you are, but the cookies are for the church bake sale so we'll need some left to sell. By the way what's for lunch?"

"Ham or turkey sandwiches, chips, apples and guess what?"

"Cookies."

"You got it. The easiest dessert to transport."

Kathleen's gaze found her son among the kids. Alone, he sat on a boulder by the lake and pitched rocks into the water. He wore a long-sleeved black shirt and black jeans. She felt hot just looking at the boy with the sun beating down on him.

"After lunch I'm going to organize a soccer game."

Jared's announcement focused her attention on him. "Oh, no. Not another sport. I hope you aren't going to expect me to play. My shoulder is stiffening up as we speak."

"I learned my lesson last time. You can be a spectator."

Kathleen released a long, exaggerated sigh. "Good. The hospital is awfully far away. Speaking of lunch —"

"We were?"

"Back a few sentences. When are we gonna eat? I worked up an appetite with all that hiking."

Jared checked his watch. "It's not even ten-thirty yet."

"Time has never played a factor in my eating habits."

"Can you wait a while longer? Give the kids time to fish, sunbathe, do some exploring."

Kathleen dug into her backpack. "Luckily I brought an energy bar." With a flourish she produced it. "Want some? I can half it."

"I ate breakfast before I left home."

"So did I. Of course, I only ate part of what I prepared. By the time I got Mark up and getting ready, the eggs had grown cold. I tossed those out. But I was able to finish the toast and orange juice."

"Mark gave you trouble about coming?"

"Actually not too much. I thought he would bring his sketching pad, but I guess he didn't."

Kathleen searched the shoreline for her son. He still sat on the boulder, his arms clasping his raised legs, his head on his knees. He stared at the water as though he were in a trance. Shane called out to him to join him, but Mark ignored his cousin.

"Maybe I can get him interested in the soccer game."

"Maybe. He used to play a lot until a few years ago. He was very good at defense."

Suddenly, Mark surged to his feet and clambered down from the boulder. With a quick scan of the area, her son headed for a grove of trees a few hundred feet from them.

He was avoiding the other teenagers and going off by himself. She'd thought when her son had agreed to come that he would participate in the activities with the others. Kathleen started forward, worry weaving through her.

Jared stopped her with a hand on her arm. "Let me talk to him. We haven't had much time to get to know each other. I'll give him a few minutes then head that way. By the time we return, we can start laying out lunch."

Biting her thumbnail, she watched Mark disappear into the shade of the trees. Part of her was relieved someone else was here to help her. But then her guilt erased the relief. She should be able to handle the situation with Mark. Until a year ago their relationship had been a good, solid one. Suddenly she felt so alone.

"Let me help, Kathleen. I owe you one. Besides, isn't that what friends are for? To help each other? I think I remember you saying something like that."

Jared's words reminded her she wasn't alone, that this man beside her might be the answer to her son's troubles, and no matter how much she wanted to deal with her son's problems all by herself, she knew when to ask for help. "Please. Maybe you can get through to him."

Jared took her hands and held them for a few seconds while his gaze delved deep into hers. A connection arced between them as though they were tied together by some invisible rope. Then, without a word, he headed toward the grove of trees. Kathleen linked her trembling fingers together as though she was praying. Yet no words came to mind. She'd forgotten how to ask God for help, wasn't sure if He would even listen to her now.

"I won't do it! Leave me alone!"

Mark's plea echoed through the dense trees and propelled Jared to a quicker pace. He scanned the dark shadows looking for the boy, but he wasn't sure which way Mark had gone.

"Go away!"

The shout, almost to a hysterical level, urged Jared to the left and deeper into the trees. His heart pounded against his chest, matching the sound of his tennis shoes pounding against the hard-packed dirt.

Who was bothering Mark? Someone in the youth group? Questions raced through Jared's mind as he raced toward Kathleen's son. He should have come sooner — not talked with Kathleen for a few extra minutes.

Pushing through some thick underbrush, Jared paused to listen for any more sounds. All that greeted him were birds chirping in the treetops and a scurrying noise behind him. Nothing else. Squinting, he searched the shady expanse before him. Finally slumped against a large elm, curled into a tight ball, he saw Mark.

Jared tore through the forest, ignoring a branch as it slapped against his chest. An eternity later he squatted in front of the teenager, his breathing coming in gasps.

"Mark, are you all right? Did someone hurt you?"

The boy remained still, only a slight tensing of the shoulders indicating that Mark might have heard him.

"Mark," Jared said more urgently.

Kathleen's son seemed to shrink into a tighter ball.

Jared's concern escalated. He laid his hand on Mark's shoulder and shook him gently. "Please let me help you."

Mark unfurled his lanky body and raised his head to spear him with half-closed eyes. "Dr. Matthews, why are you here?"

"I heard you yelling at someone. I thought maybe you were in trouble."

Mark shoved to his feet, nearly sending Jared backward. He stood, too, noting the boy's disheveled appearance; he looked almost as if he had wrestled with someone on the ground. Again Jared wondered who had been bothering Mark in the woods.

"Who were you talking to?"

Mark turned away. "No one."

"If you're having a problem with someone, maybe I can help."

"Everything's fine."

"Are you —"

"I'm hungry. When's lunch?" Mark started back toward the lake, not looking around to see if Jared followed him.

Jared let Mark go, giving him some space. He peered into the trees around him and saw no one else. Yet the boy was keeping something from him. So often teenagers think they can solve their problems alone, he thought, finally heading back toward the others. Jared made sure he kept Mark in sight at all times. It was obvious the boy had had a run-in with someone.

When Jared emerged into the sunlight, the lake only a hundred feet away, Mark was back with the others, off to the side, observing Aaron reeling in a fish. The coolness of the forest vanished to be replaced with a warmth that should have made him feel better. He didn't. Mark was a deeply troubled teen. Was it because of his father's untimely death or something else? Was he taking drugs? Or was he ill?

Kathleen strode toward him, her short auburn hair reflecting the rays of the sun, the look in her dark-brown eyes troubled. The worry etched into her features only reinforced his own concern. He wanted to help her. In the brief time he'd known her that had become important to him. Maybe if he helped her, he would feel he had atoned for not being there for Alice. Whatever the reason, Kathleen and her son were part of his life now, and he intended to discover what was wrong with Mark, then correct it.

CHAPTER FIVE

"I thought you were gonna be here a half hour ago." Laura stood to the side to allow Kathleen and Mark into her house.

Kathleen slid a glance toward her son. "It took longer to get ready than I anticipated."

"Everyone's out back, Mark," Laura said as she shut the front door.

Kathleen's son mumbled something, then, with shoulders slouched, ambled toward the kitchen. Even though the temperature promised to be in the high eighties, Mark wore black cutoff jeans and a black sweatshirt.

"He isn't swimming?" Laura whispered.

Kathleen shook her head and waited until her son disappeared into the kitchen before continuing, "He said he didn't feel like it."

"Remember when we couldn't get him out of a pool?"

"Yes," Kathleen murmured, thinking back to only two summers ago before her life had whirled out of control.

"Well, sometimes there's no second-guessing teenagers. Shane announced this morning at breakfast he had a date later this evening with a new girl in town. This is the first time he's shown any interest in the female population of Crystal Springs."

"That's pretty normal for a sixteen-year-old."

Laura started toward the kitchen, tossing over her shoulder, "Yeah, but think of all the worrying I'll be doing."

She would love to have that kind of worrying, Kathleen thought. Instead, she had to worry about whether her son was getting mixed up in something bad, like drugs. She had read up on the subject this week, hoping to educate herself in case that was the problem. But for some reason that didn't feel right.

In the kitchen, the sounds of laughter and children's loud voices came from the backyard. "My gosh, who do you have out there? The whole neighborhood?" Kathleen peeked out the window overlooking the patio and pool. Hannah ran by with Terry chasing her. Then she heard Jared's deep voice calling to them to slow down. "Laura, I thought this was going to be just the family." She faced her sister who couldn't hide the guilty expression fast enough.

"What are you up to?"

"Nothing."

"You didn't tell me Jared and his family were going to be here."

"Does that make a difference?" Laura whirled about and fidgeted with the vegetable tray, rearranging the carrot and celery sticks.

"I'm not interested in dating anyone."

"Did I say you were?" Laura straightened the carrots again.

"I know your tactics. Don't forget I grew up with you."

Laura put the last carrot down on the pile and turned. "Okay. I invited him because I think it would be wonderful if you two dated and got to know each other. He's lonely. You're lonely. His kids need a mother. Mark needs a man around."

Her sister's declaration made Kathleen's face blush. "Bad timing. I don't think he's looking and I'm certainly not. I was lucky to have such a wonderful marriage with John. A lot of people don't get even one good marriage."

"Like Jared? It was common knowledge the last few years of their marriage she was drinking a lot. That had to be hard on him even though he wouldn't talk about it."

"That's my point exactly. Neither one of

us is looking for a relationship."

"You don't think you can be that happy a second time around?"

Kathleen narrowed her eyes on her sister. "Don't play matchmaker. I have more than I can handle right now." She glanced out the window. "Are Mom and Dad here?"

"Couldn't come. Dad is playing golf and Mom is working at the church. Next time I'll have to give them more notice than twenty-four hours." Laura hoisted the tray and headed for the back door. "So it's only us, you and Jared's family. Not the whole neighborhood even if it sounds like it."

When her sister opened the door, the sounds of giggling and splashing drifted in, inviting Kathleen to join the fun. "Can I take anything out for you?"

"Nope. Everything else is on the patio table."

The second Kathleen stepped outside she felt Jared's gaze on her. His smile of greeting shot through her and curled her toes. The laugh lines that fanned out from the corners of his eyes spoke of a man who enjoyed smiling. The intensity in his gaze also underscored a man who could be very determined in what he wanted. Kathleen tore her regard from him and surveyed the commotion in the backyard. Every kid was in the pool except Mark who sat in a chair at the far end of the patio listening to CDs with his headphones on. His face glistened with sweat, but he remained clothed in the heavy black sweatshirt and black cutoff jeans.

"It's nice to see you, Kathleen," Jared said, approaching her, water dripping off his dark brown hair and running down his chest. He took a towel and dried himself. "Would you believe I haven't been in the pool? This is from all the splashing and carrying on."

Kathleen watched a water fight among Terry, Hannah and Chad, Laura's youngest. "They are a bit enthusiastic."

"A bit?" Jared quirked one brow. "I wish I had a tenth of their energy."

"I know what you mean. The things I could accomplish if I did."

"From what I've seen, you've accomplished quite a bit in a short time. Anyone who can have their house straight and in order in two weeks is amazing. I'm impressed. And on top of that you've taken my daughter under your wing." Jared looked her right in the eye and said, "You were heaven sent. An answer to my prayers."

The intensity in his regard snared her, holding her captive. Vaguely she heard the children in the pool, her sister and brother-in-law Brad talking, but none of it mattered.

Someone behind her cleared his throat then coughed, breaking the connection between her and Jared. She glanced over her shoulder and saw Brad grinning.

"Sorry. Something went down the wrong way," her brother-in-law said. "I'm gonna put the hot dogs and hamburgers on the grill. I'm taking orders now."

"A hamburger," Kathleen and Jared said at the same time.

Kathleen laughed. "I guess great minds think alike."

"Do you need any help?" Jared asked, tossing his towel onto the chaise lounge nearby. He retrieved a T-shirt and slipped it over his head.

"No, I think I can manage. You two enjoy yourselves." Still grinning as though he knew something no one else knew, Brad strode to the pool and asked each child what they wanted to eat.

Now not only was her sister matchmaking, but it appeared that her brother-in-law was in on it, too. Later she would have to have a word with both of them. She didn't need that kind of help.

"That leaves us to watch the children." Jared took a seat on the end of the chaise lounge.

Kathleen sat in the glider, her gaze trained on the pool and the five children splashing and yelling.

"Mark doesn't want to swim?"

"No."

"I guess he didn't realize that Aaron and Shane were going to be here."

"I don't think that would have made a difference. He told me he didn't like to swim anymore."

"Did he ever tell you who he was talking to in the woods?"

"He refused to discuss it with me. When I brought it up, he stomped from the room. Do you think someone is harassing him? Someone in the youth group?"

Jared leaned forward, resting his elbows on his thighs and lacing his fingers loosely together. "I hope not. I want to think no one in the group would, but he was quite upset that day. It's obvious something happened."

"Kids can be intolerant of someone different and you have to admit that Mark hasn't gone out of his way to be friends with anyone."

"They're good teens."

Kathleen sighed. "I know. I can't see anyone in the youth group harassing Mark, either."

"It's a mystery we may never solve. I'll ask around with some of the kids and see if they know anything."

"There was a time when Mark would tell me everything. Not anymore."

He straightened. "That's being a teenager. Nothing strange about that."

"I know. I just want my old Mark back."

"I would like to talk with a colleague about Mark, a psychiatrist I have a lot of faith in."

"What do you think is wrong?" Alarm bolted through Kathleen.

He leaned closer. "Change is part of life, but I think something else is going on with Mark. It could be any number of things. We need to get Mark into see me or some other doctor. My friend may be able to help me with this."

Kathleen took a deep breath, the scent of cooking hamburgers saturating the air. "Please do. If you think he can get Mark to agree to a physical that would be great."

"Then I'll talk to him and get back with you." Rising, Jared held out his hand for her. "Let's see if Brad or Laura need our help."

"And give up our lifeguarding job?" She placed her hand in his, needing to lighten the mood.

"I think Shane and Aaron can handle the little ones."

"Don't let Hannah hear you refer to her as a little one."

"That's the truth. A boy called her the other day and it wasn't because he wanted her to play soccer or baseball. I heard her giggling on the phone." He shook his head. "She wears a new dress to church, and the next day she gets a call from a boy who wants just to talk to her on the phone."

"Oh, that's nice."

Jared's eyes widened. "Nice! Not in my book. I'm not ready for Hannah to like boys. She's only twelve."

"Dr. Matthews, I've got a news flash for you. There is nothing you'll be able to do to stop it. Remember, change is part of life."

"I should have known you would throw my words back in my face," he said with a chuckle.

"At least you know I was listening."

"True." He started toward Brad and Laura, tugging Kathleen with him. "Come on. If we hurry, we can beat the kids to the food."

"Is that the last of the dishes?" Kathleen asked, stacking plates beside the sink.

"Yeah." Jared set the plates he held on the

counter. "Brad and Laura are cleaning up the mess outside. I told them we would take care of the kitchen."

"I put the movie on in the den and asked Mark to referee if things got out of hand. He didn't grumble too much."

"I'm surprised. I would have. To be left with an eight-, an eleven- and a twelve-year-old can't be a teenage boy's dream of a fun evening."

"We shouldn't be too long cleaning up in here, then we can go rescue him."

Jared surveyed the dirty dishes. "Are you sure? Doesn't your sister believe in paper plates?"

"Laura never does things the easy way. She bought this set of dishes especially for outdoor parties." Kathleen rinsed off a brightly flowered orange, yellow and blue plate and gave it to Jared to put in the dishwasher.

"Then I'm surprised she has a dishwasher. Makes life easier."

"Laura does draw the line at some things."

"Speaking of drawing, did you ever see what Mark has been drawing in his sketch pad?"

"Nothing but harmless pictures of the yard, house, a few animals."

"I wish I had a talent to draw. I barely manage stick people."

"Me, too. Mark got his talent from his dad. When creativity was being handed out, I was at the end of the line."

"Your talents lie in other directions. Your organizational abilities are wonderful and those cookies Hannah brought home that you two baked were to die for."

Kathleen inclined her head. "Thank you. I'm glad she could help me. We had fun that day."

"I know. Hannah is still talking about it."

"The ladies of the church decided to have another bake sale next month. I'll have to ask her to be my assistant again."

Jared put the last platter into the dishwasher and closed it. "Now it's my turn to thank you."

He was only a few inches away. His presence commanded her whole attention. He reached up and smoothed her hair behind her ear. Her throat clogged, she swallowed hard. No words came to mind as she stared into his blue eyes, so like the water at the lake last weekend, warm, glittering, inviting.

"You don't have to do that. I enjoy Hannah's company," Kathleen finally said, her voice husky.

He closed what little space was between them. "She's opened a bank account to save her money."

Her heartbeat increased. "That's good."

"She has several jobs lined up this week." Jared slowly bent his head toward hers.

Acute awareness charged the atmosphere. Kathleen ran the tip of her tongue over her dry lips. "She's a great work—"

A scream rent the air.

"That's Hannah." Jared spun about and raced toward the den.

Kathleen was on his heels as different scenarios zipped through her mind. The beat of her heart sped even faster. She burst into the den right behind Jared and came to a halt, nearly colliding into him. Her gaze riveted on her son standing before the busted television screen with blood dripping down his leg and onto the carpet. Mark stared at the gaping hole in the set, a dazed expression on his face. The three other children sat on the couch, their eyes wide, their mouths hanging open, huddled together.

"Take them into the kitchen. I'll see to Mark," Jared said as he moved toward the teenager.

Shocked, Kathleen didn't react for a few seconds. The children's whimpering sounds urged her forward. She hurried to the couch and drew them into her arms, hugging them to her. "Come on, let's go into the other room."

"He — he kicked the TV in." Hannah sniffed, tears running down her face. "I — I — don't know why. Everything was fine one minute, the next he —" The young girl trembled.

"Your dad will take care of Mark."

Kathleen helped the children to their feet, sheltering them close to her body. She headed for the door, glancing over her shoulder as she left the room. Mark was seated now while Jared examined his leg. Quickly she ushered the children into the hallway, her thoughts numb as though this was happening to someone else and she was just a spectator.

Laura and Brad rushed toward them. "We heard a scream. What's wrong?" Laura asked, embracing her youngest son, who was now crying.

"Mark kicked in the TV. Jared's with him right now." Kathleen directed the children to the kitchen and poured some water for Hannah, who was hiccuping. Kathleen caught her sister's look of surprise and shook her head to discourage any more questions in front of the kids.

"I'll look after them. You go check on

Mark," Laura said.

Handing the glass of water to Hannah, Kathleen said, "Thanks," and left the kitchen, almost afraid to return to the den and discover why her son would do such a thing.

When she approached the room, she drew in a deep, fortifying breath before pushing open the door. Jared must have gotten a towel from the bathroom off the den to stop the flow of blood. He looked up at her when she neared them, his eyes dark with distress.

Her own worry skyrocketed. "How bad is it?"

"There are several lacerations, but they aren't too deep. Two of them need stitches. It looks worse than it is. We can go to the hospital —"

"No!" Mark yelled, jerking away and dislodging the towel. Blood oozed again from two of the wounds.

"Mark!" Kathleen waited until she had her son's attention. "Dr. Matthews needs to take care of your leg."

"No hospitals. I won't go."

The frightened, panicked look in her son's eyes scared her. She sent a silent plea to Jared.

"We can go by my office and take care of

it there, Mark, if you don't want to go to a hospital."

Some of her son's tension eased. He nodded.

"See if Laura has some gauze I can wrap around the cuts until we get to my office."

Relieved to have something to do, she hurried from the room and found her sister in the kitchen. The three children were calm now and eating cookies and drinking milk at the big oak table in the alcove.

She pulled her sister to the side. "Jared needs some gauze. Do you have any?"

"In the children's bathroom."

"Are they okay?" Both her voice and hands shook as Kathleen reached out and touched Laura, tears swimming in her eyes. "I'm so sorry this happened. I never —"

"Shh. Don't worry. They're fine now. Hannah said he cut his leg. Is it bad?"

Kathleen turned her back on the children and swiped at the tears rolling down her face. "I don't think the cuts are too bad. That's not what is worrying me. Why did Mark do it?"

"You go take care of Mark. I'll take care of the others."

"We need to go to Jared's office. A couple of the cuts need stitches. You know how Mark feels about hospitals. He refuses to go. Gets hysterical. I'm afraid of what he'll do if I force the issue."

"We'll watch Hannah and Terry. In fact, tell Jared they can spend the night. Just get some help for Mark."

Kathleen quickly made her way to the children's bathroom and retrieved the gauze, then hastened back to the den. Kneeling in front of Mark, Jared had again applied pressure to her son's cuts with the towel. He carefully removed it and wrapped the gauze around Mark's leg, then tied it off.

"That should keep it from bleeding too much until we get you stitched up." Jared rose and extended his hand to Mark.

Her son ignored it and lumbered to his feet, moving back a few paces, his gaze darting back and forth between Jared and his mother. "No hospital. Promise?"

"I'm only taking you to my office. I have everything I need there," Jared said in a calm, soothing voice.

Kathleen was amazed at how in control Jared was, while all she wanted to do was fall apart. Her son had just kicked in her sister's television. There were so many questions she wanted to ask. But first things first. After Mark's cuts were taken care of, she needed some answers.

An hour later Kathleen followed her son

into his bedroom. He stepped over a pile of dirty clothes, flung himself on the bare mattress, and rolled over to face up. He covered his eyes with his arm.

Scanning the disarray, she tried to think of how best to start what she wanted to say. The long, silent ride to the house should have afforded her enough time to come up with something, but her thoughts were a jumbled mess — like her son's room.

Finally she sucked in a deep, bracing breath and asked, "Mark, are you sure you're all right? Do you need something for the pain?"

Lowering his arm, he stared at her, his face hidden in the shadows. Kathleen started to switch on the light when her son said, "Don't. I like the dark. I'm safer."

"Safer?"

For a long moment Mark didn't say anything. Kathleen felt his gaze drilling into her as though he were trying to figure out what was behind the question.

"He can't see me in the dark."

"He?" Alarm sent her heart racing. Sweat popped out on her upper lip, her hands clammy. "Who, Mark? Does this have anything to do with the incident by the lake?"

"He's always watching me."

Kathleen stepped closer to the bed and

saw the terror on her son's face. The same kind of numbing terror struck her, seizing the air in her lungs and holding it. Finally she breathed and asked the question she had wondered since the incident, "Why did you kick in the TV?"

"He was on the TV telling everyone my secrets. I had to stop him." Rolling onto his side, away from her, Mark curled up into a tight ball and threw an arm over his head to hide.

The shaking began in her hands and rapidly spread throughout her body. She hugged her arms to her and sat down on her son's bed. Slowly she reached out and placed her trembling fingers on his back. He flinched and bolted to the far end of the bed.

"Honey," she said in a soothing voice that matched Jared's tone earlier, "you are safe here. I won't let anyone or anything hurt you."

Mark's gaze darted from her to the window to the door then back to her. His terror transformed into horrified panic, an ashen cast to his face, his eyes so large that they were all Kathleen saw when she looked at her son.

She opened her arms and prayed Mark sought refuge in her embrace. That was all she could think to do. Her throat constricted with unshed tears as she watched him decide what he should do. Then slowly his fear evaporated to be replaced with an emotionless mask that siphoned the tension out of him. He scooted toward her and let her wrap her arms around him. Laying his head on her chest, he laughed, a high-pitched sound that sliced through Kathleen's heart to her very soul.

When his laughter evolved into tears, she held him tighter, so frightened of what she was witnessing that she could hardly hold herself together. But for her son she had to. She patted his back and whispered she loved him over and over until he calmed down. Her arms ached from the fierceness of her embrace, but she was afraid to let him go, as though if she did she would lose him forever.

"Mark, honey," she whispered into the quiet.

No response.

She pulled back. Her son's eyes were closed, his face relaxed in sleep. She laid him back on the mattress and covered him with a sheet from the floor by the bed. Standing over him, she watched him sleep, one minute slipping into another until twenty minutes had passed and the dark shadows had deepened as night crept through the window and into the room. He didn't stir the whole time.

She tiptoed to the door and eased it open. A creak sounded in the silence and sent a chill down her. She peered at Mark and sighed when she saw that he was still asleep on the bed, the light from the hallway illuminating him.

Precious memories from his childhood flooded her mind, twisting her heart into a knot. She shut the door part way, leaving it a few inches open. Turning off the hall light, she made her way toward the stairs. At the top she gripped the banister, squeezing her eyes closed as she swayed. Sinking to the step, she sat, burying her face in her hands, her body quaking.

What was going on in her son's mind? Hallucinations of a man after him? Inappropriate emotional responses? Laughing one moment, crying the next? What else? The very thought panicked her. She had so many questions and no answers.

Wearily she shoved herself to her feet and trudged down the stairs. Jared was waiting in the kitchen. She could smell the coffee brewing that he must have put on. The aroma drew her toward the heart of the house, as Jared had once called the kitchen.

She entered the room and leaned back

against the door as though it could keep her upright. All she wanted to do was collapse into the nearest chair, bury her head as her son had and forget this day had ever happened. She wished her problems would disappear that easily; she knew they wouldn't.

Jared pivoted. One look at her face and he was across the room and pulling her into the shelter of his arms. For a few seconds she felt as though she had come home. Then she remembered.

"What happened?"

"Besides my son kicking in the TV?" Hysterics threatened to take over. She squashed the feeling and leaned back to look into Jared's comforting expression. "Mark believes a man is after him."

"Believes?" Jared's brow wrinkled.

"That the man was talking to the world through the television set and exposing all his secrets. That's why he kicked the TV to stop the man."

Jared's frown deepened to a scowl. "He's hallucinating."

Kathleen nodded, the action cementing in her mind the depth of her son's problems. "I don't understand any of this. Why's this happening? Mark was always such a sweet child."

"I don't know, but we must find out."

Desperate, she latched onto the word *we* as though he had cast her a lifeline and she was going down for the third time. "What do I need to do?"

"Mark needs to go to the hospital. I know it won't be easy getting him there, but this isn't something we should deal with at my office. He needs to be watched. I need to run tests. There are a number of things that could be wrong."

"Like what?"

"I hate to speculate without more information."

"Don't tell me that." Her voice rose.

"Okay. I need to look at drug abuse, a brain tumor, thyroid and other metabolic disturbances as well as schizophrenia or manic depression, to name a few psychoses."

Kathleen had to sit, overwhelmed by all the illnesses he'd listed. Her legs shook so badly she wasn't even sure she could walk the few feet to the chair. Starting forward, she faltered. Jared clasped her to him and helped her to the seat. Her emotions frozen, she stared at the flowered mat on the glass table. The bright colors were cheerful, a sign of hope and in stark contrast to what she felt.

Jared poured them each a cup of coffee

and sat next to her. "Now you see why I hate to speculate. It could be any number of things."

She raised her tear-filled eyes. "Brain tumor. Schizophrenia." A bone-chilling cold embedded itself in her, causing her whole body to quake. She clasped her hands together but nothing stilled their shaking.

Jared scooted his chair closer until their knees touched. He gripped her upper arms and rubbed his warm hands up and down them. "I don't have to tell you his hallucinations aren't a good sign. Something is very wrong with Mark and the sooner we get him to the hospital the better."

"He was so exhausted. He just fell asleep. He hasn't done that in a while. Can we take him first thing in the morning?"

Jared offered her a smile. "That's fine since not much would be done tonight."

Kathleen reached for the mug and clutched its warmth. Slowly she brought it to her lips and drank some of the coffee. "How am I going to get Mark to the hospital? He won't agree to go. You saw how he was tonight."

"Let me come over and help. If we can't get him to go willingly, then we'll have to look at other ways."

"What did I do wrong, Jared?"

He placed his hands over hers on the mug and looked her straight in the eye. "Nothing. We can't control what happens to others. All we can do is be there for them and get them the help they need."

"Is that what you did for your wife? Is that how you handled her drinking problem?" Kathleen asked, desperate for any assistance in dealing with what was happening to her son.

Jared yanked back, his hands falling into his lap. He hung his head, staring at his third finger on his left hand. He massaged the place where his wedding ring would have been. "I tried, but I failed her."

The whispered words sent an icy bolt straight through her heart. She had opened an old wound and hadn't even known it. "I didn't mean —"

He jerked his head up. "I can help Mark, Kathleen. We'll get him the help he needs." Each word he spoke was clearly and slowly pronounced as though he was making a vow to her.

In the midst of all the swirling emotions between them Kathleen wondered if Mark and his troubles were a substitute for his wife and her drinking. Even in her distress Kathleen knew in the end that could be a problem.

Jared rose. "I'd better leave now. Get some sleep. I'll be back first thing tomorrow morning. Say about seven."

"Seven sounds fine. I doubt I'll get much sleep."

"You need your rest. You may have a long road ahead of you and you don't want to get sick yourself."

He made his way into the entry hall. Pivoting, he took her hands within his, a connection that felt so right to Kathleen.

"Call me if you need to talk or need anything else. I'm here for you." He started for the door and stopped. "Kathleen, at times like this I turn to the Bible. Seeking the word of God is always a comfort to me when I don't think I can go ahead another day."

He opened the door and disappeared before Kathleen had time to react to the anguish she heard in his voice. She didn't know a lot about his wife's problem, but Kathleen knew it had profoundly affected Jared, creating a pain in him that she wasn't sure he realized the depth of.

She touched the closed door as though that gesture would ease some of Jared's agony as he had tried to ease hers. Tears flooded her eyes and rolled down her cheeks. She pressed against the cool wood, squeezing her eyes shut.

"Got to keep busy," she muttered in the silence.

With that in mind she headed for the kitchen where she cleaned up the two mugs and a few dishes left in the sink from earlier. After putting them in the dishwasher, she switched it on, then left. Walking through the house, she checked to make sure the windows were closed and locked, as well as the doors. Anything to keep her occupied. After her brief tour, she came back to the living room and stood in the middle, slowly making a full circle as though not sure what to do next.

She spied the family Bible on the coffee table where it had always been placed in her house in Shreveport. She remembered Jared's parting advice and fingered the leather-bound book with its gold lettering. John had bought this for them when Mark had been born. His birth date was inscribed inside it.

Kathleen dug her teeth into her lower lip to keep her emotions in check. She couldn't fall apart. Too much left to do. Tomorrow would be a long, long day, even if her son went willingly to the hospital. If he didn't — she didn't want to think of that happening.

She sank onto the navy-and-maroon plaid couch and laid her hand on top of the Bible.

The warmth beneath her palm comforted her, prodding her to open its pages and seek answers. God had let her down with John. She'd begged him to spare her husband and her plea had gone unanswered. She snatched her hand away and bolted to her feet. There were no solutions in those pages for her.

Glancing at the stairs, she thought she might as well try and get some rest. At least lie down and close her eyes. She made her way toward her bedroom, stopped outside Mark's and pushed the door open, needing to see her son peacefully asleep again.

The bed and room were empty.

CHAPTER SIX

Jared walked around his empty house, listening to the quiet that rarely occurred in the Matthews household. He couldn't sleep; he couldn't even sit for long. Restless energy assailed him, prodding him to keep moving. Tonight he'd finally admitted to another that he'd failed his wife. He'd always known in his heart he had, but this was the first time he'd said it out loud.

He should have gone back to Laura and Brad's and picked up the children. Then at least he wouldn't be so alone. But he needed to be back at Kathleen's early and he hadn't wanted to disturb Hannah and Terry since they had both already fallen asleep, according to Laura, when he'd called.

Jared went out on the back patio and stared up at the crystal clear sky with thousands of stars twinkling. He would find the answers to Mark's problem. He had to. Maybe then he wouldn't be so torn up inside over Alice and his failure to help her in her time of need. Just like his younger brother all those years ago. The helplessness he'd experienced trying to breathe life into Greg after pulling him from the lake assailed Jared. He hadn't known how to revive him and when help had finally arrived, it had been too late for his little brother.

Thinking of his advice to Kathleen, he closed his eyes and murmured, "Heavenly Father, please give me the strength and knowledge to help Kathleen and Mark. Help me to find out what is wrong with Mark and to support Kathleen through this."

When he opened his eyes to the black sky a few minutes later, the restlessness in him abated. He wasn't alone. God was with him and would be there to help when the time came. Kathleen needed a friend and he would be there for her. He would show her the power of God's healing and in turn give her the means to support herself.

The ringing of the phone beckoned him inside. He hurried to it and picked it up on the fifth ring. "Dr. Matthews."

"Jared, Mark's gone."

Kathleen's panic came through the wires loud and clear. He went rigid, automatically tensing every muscle as though he were frozen. "What happened?"

"I went to check on him before I tried to

get some rest. He's not in his bedroom. I've searched the house and yard. He's not here."

"Have you called the police?"

"Yes. They are on their way, but I'm not sure there's much they can do. He hasn't been gone long and there is no sign of foul play."

"I'll be over. We need to stress to them the importance of finding him."

Even though his voice sounded calm, he fought his own sense of panic and urgency. After what had happened at Laura and Brad's this evening, he was afraid of what Mark might do next.

"I tried to, Jared."

"Then we both will try again. I'll be there in a few minutes."

He hung up and rushed to get his car keys and medical bag in case they found Mark and he needed help immediately. He remembered his prayer to God earlier. He recited it again as he went out to the garage.

Kathleen thrust open the front door before Jared had a chance to ring the doorbell. Her first impulse was to go into his arms and let him hold her. Maybe then this feeling of her life being out of her control would stop. Even though the urge was strong, she didn't. She stepped to the side and allowed Jared into her house, her grip on the door the only thing keeping her upright.

Jared pivoted in the middle of the entry hall to look at her. "Do you know any places that Mark would go in Crystal Springs?"

She shook her head, her throat tight and dry from the emotions rampaging through her.

"Does he know anyone besides your family?"

"No. Not well enough to show up on their doorstep at midnight."

"You've talked to Laura and your parents?"

She nodded. "They wanted to come over, but I told them no. I just couldn't be —" How could she tell him that he was the only one she wanted here? The revelation had stunned her when her sister and parents had offered to come be with her and she had turned them down. She still wasn't sure what to make of it. She didn't have the energy to wade through her emotions to discover why Jared had become so important to her in a few short weeks. She was afraid she was becoming dependent on him. That couldn't continue when Mark was taken care of. But for the moment she needed Jared.

He held out his hand. "Come on. Let's go into the kitchen and get some real coffee to keep us awake while we wait for the police."

Releasing her tight grip on the door, she closed it, then fitted her hand within his, the link a reminder of the strength Jared exuded. "I don't think I need anything to keep me awake. But coffee sounds good." Maybe it would warm the icy chill that held her in its clutches.

Jared led the way and seated her at the table while he went about preparing the coffee as though he lived in her house and knew where everything was. Watching him in her kitchen making something as ordinary as a pot of coffee soothed her tattered nerves. His self-assurance radiated from him and gave her hope.

When he came over to the table and sat next to her, she took a deep breath of the coffee-scented air and said, "I think Mark heard us talking about him going to the hospital."

"Why do you say that? He was upstairs. We were down here."

"I didn't realize he could hear what was going on in the kitchen from his room. The air-conditioning vent carries noises from this room to his. I heard the dishwasher going when I was checking out his bedroom earlier tonight."

"So you think he's run away, not just gone for a short time like the other evening?"

"Yes, he took his backpack and some money with him. He's gone. I know it in here." She pressed her hand over her heart, which increased its beat beneath her palm as she thought of the implications of what she'd said. "In Shreveport he didn't even take that when he ran away for the day." Her throat constricted around each word she spoke, making her voice weak and raspy. "I may never see him again, Jared."

He took her hands within his and held them tightly between them. "You will. If he's here in Crystal Springs, we'll find him."

"What if he isn't?"

"We'll find him," Jared stressed again in a vehement tone.

The sound of the doorbell cut through the tension-laden air. "That must be the police." She started to rise.

Jared surged to his feet and placed his hand on her shoulder, forcing her back onto the seat. "I'll answer it and bring them in here."

While he was gone, Kathleen noticed the coffee had stopped dripping, but she didn't have the energy to get up and pour them a cup. She stared at the glass pot with the dark brew as though it had all the answers to her problems. But nothing came to mind except more questions. What had she done wrong? Why was God letting this happen to her son?

When the door to the kitchen swished open, she peered toward Jared and the policeman who entered. The man looked no more than twenty-two. So young to find the most important person in her life. Not much older than her son, and yet she would rely on him to search for Mark.

"Would you like some coffee, Ted?" Jared asked, walking to the counter and getting some mugs down.

"That would be nice. My baby daughter has been keeping my wife and me up lately."

Jared motioned for the officer to have a seat at the table. Then Jared brought the mugs to them and set them down in front of each person. "I bet she's teething."

"Yes, sir. One in and another on its way."

Kathleen cleared her throat. "Officer, my son is missing. What are you going to do about it?" The sharp bite to her words made her regret her question the second she said it. The policeman wasn't at fault for her son's disappearance — she was.

"Sorry." Ted smiled sheepishly and took

out a pad and pen. "When did you discover your son was gone?"

"About an hour ago."

Ted looked up from writing. "Only an hour?"

"Yes, but I know he's run away. His backpack is gone. So is the money he was saving." She filled him in on Mark's strange behavior.

"May I see his room?" the officer asked when she finished.

She nodded while the officer slid her son's photograph in his shirt pocket. Standing on wobbly legs, she clasped the back of the chair to steady herself.

Jared rose and put his arm around her. "I can show Ted for you," he whispered into her ear.

"No, I'm fine." She moved from the comfort of his touch and plodded up the stairs to Mark's bedroom, her legs feeling as though she wore ten-pound weights on each one.

In her son's room the officer picked his way through the mess on the floor to the window. He opened it and looked out. "He could have climbed down from here." He backed away and searched the area.

When Ted was finished with his inspection, he came to stand in front of Kathleen. "Have you called all his friends and made sure he wasn't with them?"

"We just moved here. He doesn't know very many people, but I did check with the ones I know about."

"Where did you move from?"

"Shreveport."

"Could he try to return to Shreveport?"

Again guilt assailed her. Had she been wrong to move back home? "I don't know. Tomorrow morning I'll call everyone I can in Shreveport and let them know Mark is missing."

"That might be a good idea. In the meantime, I'll put an alert out about your son."

"Thank you, Ted. I appreciate anything you can do for Mrs. Somers."

"Sure, Doc. But there's not much I can do without any leads to go on. Mrs. Somers, if you can think of anything else, please call me at the station." Ted reached into his pocket and withdrew a card. "My number is on there."

The officer returned to the downstairs entry hall and retrieved his hat from the chair where he had laid it earlier. He shook Jared's hand and bid Kathleen a good night. She watched Jared close the door on the policeman as though she were observing the scene from afar. She needed to do something to find her son, but what?

Jared faced her, a few feet separating them. "Ted is a good man. He'll do what he can."

"That's just it. I'm not sure there's much the police can do. Runaways disappear all the time." Her voice caught on the last few words as her throat thickened.

He took a step toward her, compassion on his face. "And runaways are found, too."

"I know, but Mark isn't acting right. What if he does something crazy?" While watching Jared through the blur of tears, she swallowed several times.

"Kathleen —" Jared paused, a nerve in his jaw twitching. "Kathleen, we will find him." He covered the small space between them and drew her into his arms.

She went gladly into his embrace, seeking the support and warmth he offered. His strong arms about her held her upright while the steady beat of his heart soothed her, its rhythmic pace entrancing her.

After gathering her composure, she pulled back. "I need to do something now."

"What?"

"I'm going to drive around Crystal Springs tonight. Maybe I'll get lucky and find Mark before —" She couldn't finish her sentence. The thought of what could happen to him caused the words to stick in her throat.

"Okay. But I'm coming with you and I'm driving. I don't think you should do it alone."

She closed her eyes for a few seconds in relief. "Thank you. I was hoping you would volunteer to come."

"Look at these sketches, Laura," Kathleen said, handing her sister a pad she'd found hidden in Mark's bedroom that morning while searching for anything that would give her a hint about where her son had gone. Searches the night before last, yesterday and this morning hadn't turned up anything — not Mark, not a clue where he was.

Laura flipped through the sketch pad, her frown intensifying with each picture she saw. "Oh, my, Mark is deeply troubled. I knew something was wrong, but —" She shook her head and gave the pad back to Kathleen.

Her gaze caught the last sketch her son must have drawn. Mark was in the middle of a forest with bare trees. Hidden behind each trunk was the same dark, menacing figure staring at him. Each shapeless form had one thing that stood out: large black eyes filled with anger, all directed at Mark. Kathleen shivered and dropped the pad on the kitchen table. The thud sounded ominous in the quiet, sending a cascade of chills from the top of her head to the tip of her toes.

"It's been almost two days and nothing. What if he's hurt somewhere or —" Kathleen couldn't finish the thought. It was unbearable even to think. She pushed it away and focused on what was being done. Thanks to Jared, the police were seriously pursuing her son's disappearance. She and Jared were going to search again later that day — even though she felt they had already covered every square inch of Crystal Springs and the surrounding area. Her friends in Shreveport hadn't heard from Mark, which probably meant he hadn't gone there. If only she knew where her son was.

Laura covered Kathleen's hand on the table. "Honey, he will be coming home. He will get the help he needs. The whole church is praying for Mark's return."

"But why is this happening to my son? First he lost his father suddenly and now this —" Kathleen fluttered her hand in the air "—whatever is wrong with him."

"Let's pray for Mark. You'll feel better."

Kathleen shot to her feet. "Feel better? Prayers aren't going to bring my son home. Prayers aren't going to make me feel better.

Only Mark's safe return will do that." She began to pace the kitchen, restlessness attacking her with a relentlessness that urged her to keep moving.

When the phone rang, Kathleen jumped. She whirled and hurried to it. Maybe it was the police or the private detective she'd hired.

"Hello." Silence greeted her. Her grasp on the phone grew tighter when she heard soft breathing. "Mark, is that you?"

Still silence sounded in her ears. "Please, honey, tell me where you are. I can come get you."

"Mom —"

"Yes, Mark."

A long pause, then the phone went dead.

"Mark!" Kathleen shouted into the receiver, wishing she could renew the connection.

The second she replaced the phone on its hook, she looked at the number on the caller ID box. A 918 area code? He wasn't in Crystal Springs. He wasn't even in the vicinity. She immediately snatched up the receiver and dialed the number Mark had called her from.

On the seventh ring someone picked it up and said, "Blue Moon Café," in a deep, gruff voice.

"Who am I speaking with?"

"Lady, who do you want?"

"Is there a teenage boy with brown hair cut short there? He's five feet eight inches tall, probably wearing black jeans."

"Nope. He just left and I don't have time to chat. My break's over." The man hung up.

The dial tone droned in her ear. Shaking, she called the number again. It rang and rang. Finally Kathleen put the receiver down in frustration and spun about.

"Mark called me from a Blue Moon Café with a 918 area code. Where is that?"

Laura flipped through the phone book until she found the map of the United States with the various area codes. "Eastern Oklahoma."

"Not too far away," Kathleen whispered, trying to think what to do next. She was so tired that her mind took longer to put her thoughts together.

"If he called, that means he's okay." Laura closed the phone book with a thud.

"You keep calling this number until someone answers. Find out where the Blue Moon Café is. I'm packing."

"Packing?"

"I'm going to bring my son home."

"Let the police —"

"I can't sit here doing nothing but waiting. I must look for Mark and now I have a place to start."

"If he stays put long enough for you to find him."

Kathleen left the kitchen as her sister punched in some numbers. She ran up the stairs and threw some clothes into a bag. Ten minutes later she came back down the stairs, ready to go as soon as Laura pinpointed where the restaurant was located.

When she entered the kitchen, Laura put the phone down. "Someone answered on my fifth try. The phone is a pay phone at a café near the downtown area of Tulsa."

"Then that's where I'll be." Kathleen searched for her car keys, found them and grabbed her purse.

Laura stopped her by blocking her path to the garage. "You can't run off by yourself and look for Mark in a strange city. Let the private detective investigate."

"Yes, I can, and that's exactly what I'm going to do. I can't sit any longer and wait to hear news of my son."

"Then I'm coming with you. If you just wait a while, I'll get what I need —"

Kathleen sidestepped her sister and jerked open the door to the garage. After pressing the garage-door opener, she

138

walked to her car to stow her overnight bag. "I'm not waiting. I can't afford to lose any more time. You've got a family to take care of. I could be gone a while. I'll be fine."

Jared pulled up behind her and parked, blocking her exit more effectively than Laura had a few minutes ago. Short of ramming his sedan with hers she wasn't going any place until he moved his car.

Anger welled in her. The seconds ticked away, precious moments she couldn't afford to lose. If Mark wasn't in Tulsa when she arrived, she didn't know what she would be able to do, and it was important she be involved in finding her son.

"Please move. I'm leaving," she said as Jared approached her.

"Where are you going?"

"To find Mark in Tulsa. He called from a café fifteen minutes ago."

"Yes, Laura told me. Your sister and I don't want you to go alone."

"Well, I've got news for both of you. I'm going to Tulsa to find Mark. Period. End of discussion."

"Okay, but I'm coming with you."

"I appreciate the offer, but —"

He held up his hand to stop her protest. "I'm coming because you don't know what kind of state you'll find Mark in. If he's having a mental breakdown, you'll need help."

"I can't ask you to do that. I don't know how long I'll be gone." Frustration churned her stomach, time slipping further and further away.

He straightened, determination in his expression. "I'm coming. I told you I would do what I could to help Mark. My partner is covering for me for a few days and Laura will take care of Hannah and Terry."

"You arranged all that? When did Laura call you?"

"Fifteen minutes ago."

Kathleen glanced back at her sister who had emerged from the house. "She must have called you first."

"All we have to do is swing by my house and let me pick up a few things in case we're gone for a while."

She started to protest, saw the unyielding line of his jaw and the diamond-hard glint in his eyes, and knew his coming was for the best. What if Mark needed a doctor? Tulsa was a strange city to her. Her sister and Jared would never let her go alone, and if she stopped and thought about it long enough, she would agree with their wisdom. "Fine, but you'd better be able to pack fast."

"Ten minutes. No more." Jared headed back toward his large, metallic blue car. "I'll drive and I want no arguments there. I don't think you're up to driving two hours to Tulsa."

"You weren't gonna get an argument from me on that. I'm so tired I'd probably have us in Little Rock instead of Tulsa."

He opened the door for her on the passenger's side. "How much sleep have you been getting?"

"Sleep. What's that?"

"That's what I thought. Then I expect you to sleep on the drive to Tulsa."

When Jared rounded the front of the car and slid behind the steering wheel, she said, "I don't think I can sleep. All I dream about when I manage to doze off is Mark and what he must be going through."

He reached across the seat and brushed his forefinger under one eye. "I can give you something to help you sleep, Kathleen. You need your rest. When we get Mark back — and we will — he'll need you." He grazed the skin under her other eye. "You've got dark circles and your face is pallid."

"Gee, thanks, Doc. A gal loves to hear how pretty she is," she attempted a smile that vanished almost instantly.

"My point," he started the engine, "is that

I'm coming along not just for Mark but for you, too. I'm worried about you."

His concern swelled the constant ache in her heart. She missed having a man care about what happened to her. John had always been so good about that. "I'll be fine," she said in a hoarse voice, clearing her throat and adding, "Mark is the only one you need to be concerned with."

After Mark was found, she would have to learn to go it alone. Finding Mark was too important for her to dismiss any kind of help she could get. She would never go back to depending so much on another. It hurt too much when he was taken away.

Kathleen checked the city map that Jared had picked up at a gas station. "This is it. The café should be down this street on the left."

She glanced around at the north side's rundown buildings and the seedy landscape with tall weeds growing in vacant lots and trash littering the ground. Mark was out there somewhere — alone, sick. Thinking of all the things that could happen to him, she shuddered.

Jared pulled into a gravel lot at the side of the café and parked toward the front of the redbrick building, not far from the pay phone Mark must have used.

"It would have been so nice to find Mark standing next to the phone," Kathleen murmured, shoving open the car door even before Jared had turned off the engine.

Jared quickly left the sedan. "Slow down. Where are you going?"

"To check the number on the phone," she tossed over her shoulder. She examined the black box and saw that the number had been scratched off. She dug into her purse for some coins as Jared came up to her. "I'll call Laura and see what number pops up on the caller ID box."

When her sister answered the phone, Kathleen said, "We're here in Tulsa. What number am I calling from?"

Laura rattled off the same numbers that Mark had called from.

"I'll let you know our progress, and if we stay overnight, where I'll be. If Mark calls back, please let me know immediately on my cell phone. We might be able to get there before he disappears."

"Now that you've arranged things with the phone company, all your calls are being forwarded to my house. Take care, Kathleen. You're in good hands with Jared, and his children are enjoying themselves."

"When I return, we have a few things to

discuss." Kathleen was acutely aware of Jared standing behind her. His distinctive scent filled her nostrils, reminding her she wasn't alone in this.

"I'm glad I called Jared before anyone else today. No amount of discussing will change that, little sis. See you soon."

Kathleen carefully replaced the receiver on its hook, thinking that only a few hours before Mark had held the same phone. What had prompted him to call home? Was he in trouble? Was he frightened?

"Let's go inside and see what they say about Mark." Jared touched the small of her back.

His fingertips sent a jolt through her. Again she was vividly aware of this man's presence in her life. In a few short weeks she had come to depend on him and that scared her. Nothing was normal in her life and certainly any relationship that evolved during this time would be shaky.

She walked quickly toward the front of the café. A bell rang when she opened the door and stepped inside to air laced with the scents of coffee and grease. The dingy decor of red-and-black vinyl and the near-empty diner, even though it was close to dinner time, spoke of a restaurant barely making ends meet. Kathleen headed straight for the counter next to the cash register. A man stood behind it with a dirty white apron on and a toothpick stuck between his lips.

Kathleen removed Mark's picture and shoved it toward the man behind the counter. "Have you seen this person?"

"Nope."

"Is there anyone else who works here?"

"Just me and Danny. We own this place."

"May I speak with Danny please?"

"Are you gonna order something?"

Kathleen started to say, "No," when she saw the stubborn look in the man's eyes. Instead she said, "Yes, a glass of iced tea please. Now, may I speak with Danny?"

The man peered from her to Jared, grumbled something under his breath and scuffled toward the back. He returned a minute later with a glass of iced tea and an older man with bushy gray hair following him. The first man set the glass in front of Kathleen along with the bill.

The gray-headed man asked, "You need to speak to me?"

"Yes. Have you seen this person around here? He made a call from the pay phone outside the door about three hours ago." Kathleen laid the picture on the counter.

"Yep. What did he do?"

"Ran away from home. Do you know

where he went?"

The man shook his head slowly as though he were thinking. "He ran off like someone was after him. We get a lot of transients in these parts. Here one day. Gone the next."

"Where might someone like him go in Tulsa?"

The man scratched his head, his mouth twisted in a grimace. "Maybe downtown. There are a couple of shelters around. Course, this is summer, so not much need for shelter like in winter. But it can get awfully hot. Some of them hang out at the public library, places like that."

Without touching her tea, Kathleen removed some money from her purse and paid for the drink. "Thank you. If he comes back, will you call this number and let me know?"

The old man grabbed up the twenty dollars she left for the tea. "Sure, lady."

Jared escorted her out of the café. She felt the two owners' gazes on her back the whole way to the door. Outside she took a deep breath of the hot, summer air and felt much better.

"You know you'll never hear from them."

"Probably not, but just maybe I will if Mark returns. At least we have a few places we can search."

"First let's find a hotel and get some dinner. Then we can start looking."

"But —"

He placed his fingers on her mouth. "Shh, Kathleen. You have to eat and we'll both need some sleep tonight unless we get lucky and find Mark right away."

Her lips tingled from his touch. She sighed, knowing he was right, then nodded. "Let's get a hotel downtown so we can walk the streets tonight."

"Thank goodness I came with you. You know how dangerous it would be for you to walk the streets at night by yourself."

"But I have you."

He gave her an intense look. "Yes, you have me."

CHAPTER SEVEN

"We should be out looking for Mark," Kathleen said the second the waitress left their table at the restaurant.

"And we will be just as soon as I get some food in you. Otherwise, I'm not sure you'd be going too far."

She smiled, a fleeting upturn of her mouth. "Is that your roundabout way of saying I don't look too good?"

Jared took in her ashen features, dark circles under her large brown eyes and the tight set to her shoulders. Exhaustion clung to her like a second skin, and yet she wanted to walk the streets of downtown Tulsa searching for her son, just as she had done when she had thought Mark was in Crystal Springs. His admiration grew for her every time he was around her.

"I look that bad?"

Kathleen's question pulled him from his musings. He shook his head. "Under the circumstances I think you're doing terrific. We won't be long. The waitress said she'd put a rush on our order."

"I shouldn't feel guilty taking the time to eat, but I do."

"Guilt is a mighty strong motivator."

Kathleen cocked her head, her expressive eyes turning darker. "Are you speaking from experience?"

Her question took him by surprise. "This isn't about me."

"The few things you've said in the past have left me with the impression you feel responsible for your wife's problems."

He ran his finger along the rim of his water glass. "Not her problems so much as I feel I should have been able to help her."

"Weren't you the one who said we can't control others, only ourselves?"

"I'm a doctor. I couldn't heal her."

"Did she want to get well?"

He shrugged. "Sometimes I thought she did, but then she'd start drinking again."

"And things were taken out of your hands?"

"Yes, exactly."

The waitress placed their bowls of spaghetti in front of them along with a basket of piping hot, freshly made bread.

Jared waited until the woman had left before continuing. "I thought I was doing all the right things, but in the end I guess I wasn't."

Kathleen covered his hand with hers. "Hey, just because you were doing what you were supposed to be doing doesn't mean the other person was. I have some experience in that. I couldn't control what happened to my husband, and I'm quickly finding I'm also not able to control what's happening to Mark."

"Listen, let's make a deal. For the duration of this meal, let's concentrate only on happy thoughts. Our problems can wait until we're finished eating. A deal?"

"I wish it were that easy."

"Sure it is. All you have to do is agree." He grasped her hand to shake.

"A deal, then," she said with a laugh.

The sound of her laughter reached into his heart and touched a place he'd thought frozen. His experience with Alice had robbed him of any desire for a relationship with another woman, and yet — He shoved the thought from his mind. Too much was occurring right now to let that thought grow.

"When I called Hannah this evening, she was on the line with a boy. I guess I should be lucky she even answered the phone. I got the distinct impression she wanted me to call back later. It doesn't take long for a father to become second in his daughter's life." He exaggerated a sigh while twirling his spaghetti using a fork and spoon.

"You'll always have a special place in your daughter's heart."

"Talking from experience?"

"Yes, my father is wonderful. He's always there when I need him."

"Do you need him as much as you did when you were a little girl?"

"Well, no, but the fact I know he's there gives me strength."

"Family is important."

"I agree. I wanted more children, but we didn't have any more."

"I come from a small family. When Alice and I married, we talked about having four children." He paused, remembering those early days when he didn't know about his wife's drinking problem. Even then he'd felt something wasn't quite right. "Under the circumstances, I'm glad we didn't, but I'd still like more children." He lifted his shoulder in a shrug. "I guess that's why I took on the youth group — instant family."

"Have you thought about moving back to where you grew up to be with your family?"

Jared added some more Parmesan cheese to his spaghetti. "No, I think of Crystal Springs as my home now. Besides, my parents moved to Florida. My oldest brother still lives in my hometown. My youngest died when I was a teenager. He was the reason I wanted to become a doctor."

"I'm sorry about your brother. How did he die?"

"He drowned while we were swimming at the lake. I tried to help. I couldn't."

"Oh, Jared," Kathleen murmured, her voice husky, thick.

"It was a long time ago," he said, trying to dismiss the subject before memories overwhelmed him. For a brief flash he remembered the desperation, the vow —

Silence stretched between them. Jared locked his past away, determined not to go there. He couldn't change it.

"We don't have a large family, either, but they all live in or around Crystal Springs." Kathleen glanced off in the distance. "Without them I don't know how I'd have gotten —" Her voice faded into silence. She swallowed hard and shook her head. "Summer is sure setting in fast. One day it's cool and the next it's blistering hot." She took a bite of her spaghetti and meatballs.

Jared chuckled. "So we've come to this. Discussing the weather." Breaking off a piece of a hard roll, he buttered it and popped it into his mouth.

"I thought weather would be a safe enough topic."

"We could always talk about politics or religion."

"Oh, no. I'm not going there. You drove. You're my ticket home."

"I doubt we differ too much on either subject."

Kathleen arched a brow.

"We go to the same church. How different can we be?"

She dropped her gaze to her half-empty bowl and moved the spaghetti around in circles. "I have a confession to make. I'm only attending church because my family expects it. If I still lived in Shreveport, I probably wouldn't be attending." She lifted her eyes to look deeply into Jared's. "I'm going through what you would call a crisis of faith and what Mark is going through only confirms my present feelings. I don't understand God. I didn't when John died. Mark has already been through enough. He lost his father last year, and now something is terribly wrong with him. How can God do this to my son?"

"I can't begin to tell you I know everything God has planned for us. I don't even always know the reasons behind what happens. But I do know God is always with us

153

and that His love is a powerful healing tool if you let it into your life. On Earth God never promised us a paradise. This isn't a perfect world, but His strength helps us get through the trials and tribulations thrown at us."

Kathleen drank some of her water. "It's one thing for me to go through trials and tribulations, but to have to watch my son deal with something like a brain tumor or depression or whatever is wrong with him is too much. It should have been me, not Mark. If I could trade places, I would."

Jared signaled to the waitress for the bill. "I think all parents feel that way when something happens to their child. When we find Mark, he'll need you more than ever. You'll need to draw your strength from somewhere or you'll end up depleted. Let God be there for you."

The waitress left the bill on the table. Jared took some money from his wallet and paid it, then rose, holding out his hand for Kathleen.

"Let's go look for Mark while it's still light outside."

Kathleen glanced at her watch. "We have about an hour of daylight left."

"Tomorrow we can get a list of shelters and make the rounds there, but I have a feeling he hasn't gone to one. He looks too young for them not to question him."

"He took some money with him, but he'll run out soon. How's he going to eat?"

Jared guided Kathleen from the restaurant, which was two blocks from the heart of downtown Tulsa. "We'll find him before that."

With Jared walking beside her, Kathleen felt hope. He took the photograph from her purse and began showing it to anyone they passed on the street. They had covered a good part of the downtown area by the time darkness settled over the city. And not one single person had recognized her son's picture. Doubt gnawed at her hope.

Jared turned back toward the hotel. "This is only the first night. It's late. We'll get up early tomorrow and start asking around right after breakfast."

"You're going to make me eat breakfast?"

"Yep. And you better get a good night's sleep, too. Doctor's orders."

"Yes, sir." She saluted him before pushing open the glass door into the lobby.

"If I didn't know better, I'd think you were mocking me," he said, following her into the hotel.

She turned and walked a few steps backward. "Oh, no. Never."

"Now I know you're mocking me."

155

She stopped in the middle of the large lobby. "Okay, maybe just a tiny little bit." She held her thumb and forefinger up to indicate an inch.

He closed the space between them, capturing her hand within his. "Just for that you'll have to eat an extra big breakfast tomorrow."

"Oh, no, not that." Laughter tinged her voice.

His fingers still held hers, warm and strong. Suddenly in the middle of the lobby Kathleen felt as if they were the only two people in the whole twenty-floor hotel. Voices faded. He filled her vision, his aftershave the only thing she could smell. With his blue eyes sparkling with amusement, his dimples appeared in his cheeks.

"I love your laughter," he said, his voice husky.

I love your eyes, your kindness, she wanted to say, but the words wouldn't come out. All she could do was stare into those fathomless depths and count herself lucky she had found a friend like Jared.

His expression sobered. "All kidding aside, you do need to get a good night's rest and we will be eating a big breakfast tomorrow."

"You can be very demanding, can't you?"

"Doctors learn that the first year of med school." He released her hand and slipped his arm about her shoulder. "Come on. I'll walk you up to your room, then I'm hitting the fitness room."

She twisted about and looked up into his face. "Now you *are* kidding."

"Nope. I'm not nearly ready for bed."

"I've always heard that doctors are the worst patients. What about your advice to me? Shouldn't that be good for you, too?"

"Probably. But I can function on a lot less sleep than you."

"Who says?" Kathleen punched the up button at the elevator.

He cupped her face and searched her features. "Your eyes, your expression, the tired lines about your mouth. Should I go on?"

"No, I get the point."

The elevator swished open and she stepped into it. When the doors closed, she was alone with Jared and very aware of the man beside her. She still felt the warmth of his touch on her face. She could come to care for this man very much if she wasn't careful. All she had to do to squelch that was to remember the painful months since her husband's death.

At her floor, Jared walked with her toward her room. Even though it was only ten o'clock, the silence in the hall reinforced the feeling that she and Jared were the only two people in the hotel.

At her door she turned. "I'd like to start early. I'll meet you downstairs for breakfast at seven."

He grinned, the lines on his own face indicating he wasn't immune to exhaustion. "I'll be there with my walking shoes on."

"I want to find a printer who can make up some flyers of Mark. We can hand them out when we are searching. Maybe someone will recognize his picture even later on and call. I'll put my cell number on the flyer just in case."

"We'll work something up over breakfast so you won't feel like you're wasting your time by eating. Good night, Kathleen." Jared started back toward the elevator, glanced over his shoulder and added, "Get some sleep."

She unlocked her door and slipped inside her room. Kicking off her shoes, she collapsed onto the bed, staring up at the white ceiling. Jared's last comments about guilt came to mind. He knew it was a powerful motivator — because of his own past with Alice.

Dropping her large purse by her feet,

Kathleen sat on the bench by the Arkansas River running through Tulsa. The sun sank below the trees that lined the river park. She removed her tennis shoes and kneaded first one foot then the other.

"Thank goodness I ate a big breakfast and lunch. I didn't know I could walk so much in one day," she said, scooting over so Jared could sit down next to her when he approached her. "Any luck that way —" she gestured toward the south "— because I didn't have any." She heard the edge of defeat creeping into her voice and wanted to push it away. But she couldn't, not after spending hours walking and talking to everyone she saw. She felt as though she had met every person who lived in Tulsa.

"What if Mark is no longer in Tulsa?" Kathleen asked, the question she had suppressed all day surfacing.

"Since he called you yesterday from here, this is the best place to start. We checked the bus station. He hasn't left by bus and there is no train service." Jared shifted on the bench. "We'd better be heading back. We've covered a lot of ground today."

"Yeah, we have a long walk back."

He watched her massaging her feet. "We can always see if we can find a taxi."

"No. Let's take a rest and then walk back.

We might see someone who knows where Mark is." Even as Kathleen said the last sentence, she felt the defeat grow stronger. Searching for her son was like searching for a needle in a haystack — a large haystack when she glimpsed the tall buildings jutting up toward the sky. She estimated they were a good six or seven miles away.

"I don't want to be out too late. This downtown shuts up after everyone goes home from work."

"But the people who are out at night are the very people we need to talk to."

A man and woman jogged past them on the exercise path, sweat rolling off them. The sun going down only alleviated the high temperature a little. Kathleen removed a handkerchief from her purse and dabbed at her own sweat that left a film of moisture on her face.

"Then in that case, Kathleen, only ten more minutes."

"Why, Dr. Jared Matthews, you are a hard taskmaster."

"I can rise to the occasion when I need to."

The grin that accompanied his words caused her breath to catch. "I think I've fulfilled the next six months' quota for exercise all in one day."

"I've got news for you. It doesn't work that way."

"Oh, rats —" she snapped her finger "— I was hoping it did."

Kathleen slid her shoes on her feet and tied the laces. When she straightened, she looked at Jared with his eyes closed, a calm expression on his face. His endearing features urged her to touch him. Her arm rose as though it had a will of its own, and she started to brush a wet lock of dark hair from his forehead. His eyes snapped open. She gasped and dropped her hand into her lap, as though she had been caught doing something she shouldn't.

Their gazes locked, and Kathleen's entire focus centered on the man beside her, a man who had trudged all over the downtown area with her today in ninety-plus-degree heat, handing out flyers and talking to anyone who would listen. Her heart expanded with an emotion she didn't want to acknowledge. In the midst of all her troubles, she had found something sweet and precious.

He brought his hand up to smooth damp tendrils behind her ear. The graze of his fingertips across her cheek attuned her to him. His electric blue eyes half closed as if he had just awakened from an afternoon nap. The long length of his dark lashes. The fullness of his lips tipped in a half grin. His hair that tended to curl when slightly wet. His probing regard delved deep into her heart. Their silent, tentative bond strengthened in that moment, their recent shared experiences cementing it.

"When we get back to Crystal Springs, you're going to have to go jogging with me."

"I used to jog. Haven't in months," she murmured, transfixed by the man next to her.

"You could start again. That'll get you into shape." He trailed his finger down her jawline.

She wanted to melt against him. "When I said I wanted something to do with my time, I wasn't thinking about jogging. Maybe a sit-down type activity." Her voice was breathless as though she had been jogging for miles.

He rose in one fluid motion, pulling her to her feet, the surreal moment evaporating like a mist on a hot day. "It'll be dark before we know it. We'd better start back."

They began their trek back to the hotel in silence, but Kathleen was very aware of everything Jared did even though she kept her gaze trained ahead. When his arm brushed up against hers, she nearly jumped. Her nerves were strung tight, not all due to her son's disappearance.

"Let's walk back a different way." Kathleen shifted her purse to the other shoulder.

"How about this street?" Jared pointed toward a major thoroughfare and took her hand to run across the intersection before the light changed.

As they neared the hotel, Kathleen continued to hand out flyers, but the people downtown had thinned as night approached. Total darkness fell before they reached their destination. Scanning the shadows caused goose bumps to rise on her skin, and she shivered in the warm, summer air.

"We only have a few more blocks." Jared reached for her hand again and linked his fingers through hers.

"Mark's out here somewhere," Kathleen said, staring down an alley where the lights from the street didn't penetrate. Her imagination began to run rampant. She twisted away from the alley, pushing her thoughts away.

She started to say something else to Jared when someone flew out of the blackness, grabbed her purse and ran down the street. She caught herself before falling to the pavement. With one quick glance at her to make sure she was all right, Jared was instantly after the man, dogging him as he dashed between two parked cars and headed for another alley on the other side of the street. Before the purse snatcher made the alley, Jared leaped forward and tackled him to the sidewalk.

Kathleen searched up and down the broad avenue for assistance, but it was deserted. Hoping she might be able to help Jared in some way, she hurried across the street, her heart pounding against her chest. Rounding a car, she saw him yank her purse from the man's clutches while the robber tried to scramble away. Seeing his prize gone, the purse snatcher darted down the darkened alley. Jared started after him.

"Don't!" Kathleen called out.

He stopped and spun about, his chest rising and falling rapidly. His blue polo shirt was torn and dirt smudged his cheek. There was a wild look in his eyes as Kathleen came up to him. By the time his breathing slowed, the fierceness in his expression eased.

"He could have hurt you." He clasped the purse to his chest. "I'll take care of this the rest of the way back to the hotel."

Kathleen brushed her fingers across the streak of dirt on his face. "He could have hurt *you*. Are you all right?"

"Yes. Are you?"

"Yes. Now I am. You shouldn't have gone after him. What if he'd —" She couldn't finish the sentence. The thought of what could have happened to Jared if the man had had a weapon stole her words and gripped her in a mind-numbing fear. She was the reason he was here.

One corner of his mouth lifted. "To tell you the truth, I didn't think. I reacted. If I'd thought it through, I probably wouldn't have chased after the man. Not a smart move."

With trembling fingers, she finished wiping the dirt from his face. "Well, don't next time."

"There won't be a next time. You're going to leave your purse back at the hotel. We'll carry what we need in our pockets." He guided her across the street and quickened his pace, continually scanning the area. "Let's get back to the hotel."

"You won't get an argument from me."

"Good. Nice to have an agreeable partner."

The word *partner* sounded wonderful coming from Jared. Again it reinforced the feeling that she wasn't alone dealing with Mark's problem. No matter how much she wanted not to depend on another, she knew when she was in over her head and needed help. She wasn't too proud to ask for assistance when her son's health was at stake.

Her cell phone rang as they turned the corner where the hotel was. The bright lights from the lobby loomed before them. Stopping in a well-lit area, Kathleen delved into her purse and flipped open the phone.

"Kathleen, Mark just called," Laura announced with no preamble.

"He did? Did he say anything?"

"No, but I heard him crying."

"Crying?" Kathleen's chest constricted with emotions she couldn't keep tamped down. "Do you know where he's calling from?"

"Yes, the Brady Street Shelter."

"We went there earlier today and left a picture. Did you talk with anyone there?"

"Yes. I called back after Mark hung up. The man that answered didn't know anything about Mark. The phone was in a back office. No one was supposed to be in there."

Kathleen's lungs felt tight, as though they held her breath trapped and wouldn't let it go. She determinedly inhaled and exhaled several times before saying, "We'll visit right now. Maybe he's still around. Thanks, Laura."

"Let's take the car," Jared said the second Kathleen disconnected. Without waiting for a reply, he headed for the parking garage next to the hotel.

Ten minutes later Kathleen hopped out of the car the second Jared came to a stop in the parking lot next to the shelter. She hurried toward the building with Mark's picture in hand. Jared jogged up behind her as she pushed through the front door.

The large room where meals were served was nearly empty except for a man behind the serving line, wiping down the counters, and several at a table playing a card game. Kathleen headed for the older man behind the counter.

"Excuse me, sir."

The balding man turned toward her and began to clean the counter in front of her. "Can I help you?"

"Have you seen this teenager?" Kathleen held up Mark's photo, her trembling hands sweaty, her heart hammering against her chest.

"Nope," he continued to wipe, "but I've seen that photo up in the office."

"My son called from this building not twenty minutes ago. He was here."

"I've been in the kitchen cleaning up. Maybe Vance knows something. He's back there." The old man pointed toward a hallway.

Jared laid his hand on her shoulder and squeezed gently. "Thanks. If you see him, he needs medical help. Call the number on the flyer."

Kathleen rushed toward the back office. If only Mark were sitting in there waiting for her. *God, please, please help my son. I have to find him. Get him some help before it's too late.*

The door to the office was ajar. She knocked on it and waited, her whole body quivering. Her son was close. Only twenty minutes away at the most.

"Yes?"

Kathleen stepped into the office as a man who must be Vance glanced up from the paper he was writing on. "Have you seen this person?" Again she showed her son's photo, the motion becoming second nature to her.

"No, but I have it posted over there." He waved his hand toward a bulletin board with some other people's pictures tacked up on it.

"He used the phone in here to call long distance twenty minutes ago." Kathleen felt the clock ticking, each minute of delay taking her son further away from her.

"Oh, that one. A lady just called about

him. When I was coming back here to do some paperwork, someone darted out of my office and out the emergency exit at the end of the hallway. There wasn't anything in here to take so I wasn't —"

"Thank you," Kathleen cut in and spun about.

She ran toward the back door, desperate not to waste anymore time. A beep sounded when she opened it and stepped out into the warm summer air. She scanned the area littered with several cans overflowing with trash. The stench overpowered her. She covered her nose and mouth with her hand and moved toward the field behind the shelter. Light from a street lamp illuminated only a few feet into the weed-infested lot. The rest was pitch black, and she felt as though she had hit a dark barrier.

Jared came up behind her. "Let's check the area, and if we don't find him, get some help from the police. He can't be too far."

Kathleen thought of all the places he could hide in the dark and her desperation turned to panic. Taut with tension, she peered over her shoulder at Jared. "He's out there. I can feel it."

Jared took her hand. "Then we'll find him — together."

Lord, please give me my son back. The

words whispered through her mind and peace allayed her fears, as though God had laid his hands upon her shoulders. "Together."

Kathleen walked toward the empty lot behind the shelter and beyond, beginning to make out shapes and outlines as her eyes adjusted to the dark. Some homeless people were settling down for the night. Was Mark among them?

With Jared by her side, she moved toward the cluster of people. An old man stared at them approaching, but he didn't leave. He sat on a log, drinking from a tin cup. She remembered the purse snatcher earlier and quaked.

"Do you want the police to do this?" Jared whispered into her ear.

"No police. Mark's here. That'll scare him off for sure." She strode past the man on the log, the hairs on her nape tingling.

Several people were curled on the ground, sleeping. One was inside a large cardboard box. Then Kathleen caught sight of a figure about her son's height and shape sitting against a utility pole. In the dark she couldn't tell if it was Mark or if the person was sleeping or watching her. With breath held she started toward the pole.

The person's chin rested on his chest, his

shoulders hunched as Mark's often were. Ten feet away. Five. The pounding of her heart drowned out all other sounds, its roar echoing through her mind like a freight train barreling down the tracks out of control.

CHAPTER EIGHT

"Mark?"

The person, who on closer inspection was a male, didn't move. She could tell from what little moonlight there was that he wore dark pants — possibly jeans — and a dark shirt — like her son. Was he asleep? Was he — she refused to think beyond that.

"Mark," she said in a strong voice that carried through the litter-cluttered lot.

The figure sitting against the pole stirred, slowly lifting his head and regarding her emotionlessly. Even though he was still cast in the shadows of night, Kathleen knew it was Mark. She rushed forward the few remaining feet and knelt beside him.

"Mark, it's Mom." She grasped his arm. "Are you all right?"

Mark didn't jerk away; he didn't do anything. He just sat there motionless, as though frozen in time.

"Mark?" All her fear and panic laced that one word. Why wouldn't he say something? She took hold of his other arm, commanding his full attention, her face thrust close to his. "Are you hurt?" She searched the dark shadows cast over his features for any sign her son was even hearing her.

An eerie silence prevailed. Kathleen glanced back at Jared. "What's wrong? He's not responding."

Jared squatted on the other side of Mark. "Let's get him to the car."

At the sound of Jared's voice, Mark whipped his head around and stared at him. "No hospital."

"Honey, we just want to take you back to Crystal Springs. You don't belong here."

Mark jerked his head back toward her. "No hospital. They will find me there."

The frantic desperation in her son's voice eroded her composure she had so painstakingly erected. "I'll keep you safe, but you need to come with us." With a shudder Kathleen scanned the area, the darkness looming menacingly before her. "This place isn't safe for you."

"Not safe?"

"No, Mark. My car is over there. You will be safe in it," Jared said, slowly placing his hand on the boy's arm, his voice pitched low, soothing.

"I have to be safe. I can't let them get me."

"They won't, honey. I won't let them." Kathleen rose, coaxing her son to stand with Jared's assistance.

"Mom?"

"Yes, honey."

"Mom?" he asked again, as though he wasn't sure she was his mother.

The thought that her son couldn't recognize her sent a stab of pain through her heart that nearly doubled her over. With a hidden well of strength, she supported his lanky frame as they started for Jared's car. "Mark, you are safe now." She repeated that sentence the whole way to the blue sedan, parked under a street lamp.

The light illuminated her son's unkempt appearance. From the odors emanating from Mark, Kathleen didn't think he had washed since he'd left home three days before. Even his hands were crusted with grime, dirt under his fingernails. His messy hair looked as if he had raked his hand repeatedly through it or torn at it.

Jared opened the back door and with his help Mark climbed into the car. Kathleen followed, sitting next to her son, afraid to take her eyes off him in case he disappeared again. She slid her arm about him and he laid his head on her shoulder, seemingly calmed by her continual reassurances.

After Jared started the engine and pulled out onto the street, he said, "I'll swing by the hotel and get our things. Will you be okay in the car by yourself?"

"I think so," she answered, not really sure if she would be. She didn't know what to expect from her son anymore. But that didn't matter right now. She handed Jared her room key.

"I'll be quick." Jared parked in front of the hotel and hurried into the lobby.

Kathleen noticed he took his keys with him and locked the doors before leaving. Rubbing her hand up and down Mark's arm, she murmured over and over in a pacifying voice, "You're safe, Mark. No one will hurt you."

Life continued around her, people passing the car to go into the hotel or on down the street, the bellman opening a taxi door for a woman. Ordinary, everyday activities while she held her son and tried not to breathe too deeply of his rank scent of day-old sweat and something else she didn't want to identify. She didn't want to think what he had been doing for the past few days. She wished she could blank her mind, but emotions churned inside her. She rapidly moved from relief at finding Mark to fear of what the future would bring. Something was terribly wrong with her son, and she and Jared had already agreed that Mark would go to a psychiatric hospital in Crystal Springs.

She thought of her prayer earlier to the Lord. *Thank You, heavenly Father, for bringing Mark back to me. Now what do I do?*

Kathleen stared out the window at the beautiful July day, the sun bright, the sky a clear, light blue. Looking at the landscape she felt a sense of serenity. Until she remembered. Behind her lay her son in a hospital bed, sedated after nearly tearing the place apart when he realized he was at a hospital.

She closed her eyes and could still see the picture of Mark, yelling and flailing his arms as he tried to escape. Three orderlies had been needed to subdue him. She was still amazed she and Jared had been able to get him into the building before he had come fully awake and aware of his surroundings. If not, she shuddered to think what he would have done or where he would have fled in the parking lot.

A hand settled on her shoulder and kneaded her tight corded muscles. Jared. She knew his touch, had become so used to it these past few days while waiting to see what was wrong with Mark. She wanted to lean back against his strength but instead forced herself to turn toward Jared. She had to stop depending so much on him.

"Where's Dr. Martins? Is he through?"

"Yes. I told him I would like to talk to you first."

"Oh, that doesn't sound good at all. Of course, I knew it wouldn't be something simple, but —" She couldn't finish her sentence. Her throat closed as though a fist was jammed in it.

"Let's sit down." Jared gestured toward the two-seated couch.

"Now, you really have me worried." She attempted a light tone that failed miserably.

After sitting next to her, Jared captured her hands within his. She couldn't quell the trembling that was fast spreading throughout her body. She glimpsed her son lying for the time being peacefully in the bed and wished she could take his pain away, wished she could trade places with him.

Licking her dry lips, she asked, "What's wrong?"

Jared took a deep breath as though arming himself before telling her. Her pulse quickened, her chest expanding with an incredible pressure.

"Kathleen, Dr. Martins has confirmed

what I suspected. He feels Mark is suffering from paranoid schizophrenia."

For a moment Kathleen was sure she hadn't heard right. Her mind went blank. The room tilted. She closed her eyes and still her world spun like a kaleidoscope gone crazy.

"Kathleen?"

Jared's worried voice pierced through her fog, pulling her back. The tightness about her chest constricted, making each breath she dragged in painful.

"Kathleen, I'm sorry. The changes you've seen in him over the past six or eight months plus all the tests we ran to rule out other health concerns lead us to believe he has schizophrenia."

The last word echoed through her mind, demanding she pull herself together. She opened her eyes and saw the concern etched in Jared's features, the compassion that darkened his blue gaze. A fragile dam held her emotions in check.

"I wish I could tell you something better, but he had a psychotic episode at Laura's when he kicked in the TV. His hallucinations then and later support that diagnosis. As you know these past few days we ran many tests to rule out other causes for that kind of behavior and they came up negative."

"He isn't on drugs?"

"No, and there is no brain tumor or metabolic disturbances."

"Schizophrenia," she said slowly, as though Jared had pronounced a death sentence for her son. Emotions held at bay suddenly flooded her, stealing her breath, her thoughts.

She yanked her hands from his grasp and hugged her arms to her, a chilling cold permeating itself deep into her bones. It just wasn't possible. Not her son. This can't be happening. She began to shake, her teeth chattering as though a north wind swirled through the room.

Jared slipped his arm about her shoulders and drew her against him. "Kathleen, in the past years there have been new medicines developed that are so much better than the old ones. A person with schizophrenia can live a relatively normal life, especially since I think we caught Mark's early. The earlier the better. We can get him the help he needs. Through the right medicine and psychotherapy he will be all right."

Kathleen heard Jared's words as though he were talking to her through a long tunnel. One part of her brain registered what he was saying, the other part observed the scene as a bystander would, detached, unemotional.

She couldn't think of anything to say. The process of even thinking seemed too much at the moment.

Jared's other arm enclosed her in a tight cocoon of comfort. Laying her head on his chest, she listened to his steady heartbeat, his familiar scent a balm that sought to soothe her shredded nerves.

But nothing really helped for long. Slowly the reality of the situation gripped her and tears rose from the depths of her sorrow to flow. "Why is this happening? I don't understand."

"We will get through this, Kathleen. I promise."

The vehemence in his voice reached through the haze that clouded her mind. She straightened and looked at him through the blur of tears. In that moment she realized she cared for this man a great deal, too much to handle on top of everything else. She closed her eyes, needing to block the sight of his endearing features. Tears leaked out.

The soft brush of his fingers under her eyes brought more tears to her. His kindness, his tenderness unraveled her composure further.

"You are not alone," Jared murmured and drew her against the cushion of his shoulder. "I am here. Your family, but most importantly God is with you."

She remembered her ardent prayers to the Lord. Yes, she had found her son, but why was he suffering so much? What kind of God caused this to happen to His children? "I don't understand, Jared, how God can do this to Mark. He was — is a good kid."

"Sometimes we have to put our faith in God even when we don't understand the reasons behind what happened."

"A test of our faith?" Through the sheen of tears Kathleen watched her son sleeping on the bed. Her heart broke at the sight. When Mark was sedated, he was peaceful. But when he was awake, the demons returned to plague him.

"Possibly. Jesus is our salvation. That is a promise from the Lord. Other things are negotiable."

She recalled the peace she'd felt after her prayer in Tulsa. Could she turn her life totally over to the Lord? Could she turn Mark's life over to Him? She wasn't sure that was possible anymore.

"Somehow I feel I've let my son down, that I could have stopped all this from happening. Am I being punished? Is that why my son is suffering? Because of me?"

"The Lord doesn't work that way and you

can't control everything and everyone around you."

Kathleen pulled back, twisting so she could face Jared. "You really feel that way?"

He nodded, grasping her hands and holding them between them. "You are a good mother who has stood by her son through some rough times. There are simply some things that are out of our control. We can't be responsible for the actions of others, only ourselves."

"Then why do you blame yourself for your wife's death?"

Jared blinked, surprise registering on his face. He opened his mouth to say something but snapped it closed. He glanced away. A myriad of emotions flickered across his features with finally a wounded look settling in his eyes.

"She had the drinking problem. She chose to drive while under the influence."

His eyelids slid closed. Drawing in a deep breath, he released it slowly, a ragged sound. "I'm the one who pushed her over the edge that day she drove."

Kathleen felt his tension in his tight grip, the lines of anguish carved into his expression, the quick rise and fall of his chest. "How?"

When he looked at her again, his eyes

were a stormy blue, his mouth pinched into a frown. "Because I took the keys to her car away. Because I treated her as a child, telling her she couldn't drive until she stopped drinking. I had reached the end of my patience and didn't know what else to do. She had come home with the smell of alcohol on her breath and wanted to take the kids out for dinner. I told her no and stormed from the room. I couldn't stay in the same room with her. My anger at her was so strong that day. I should have been able to control that, my reaction to her problem." He shivered as though he were reliving every awful minute of that day.

"You did what you had to do." She sandwiched his hands between hers.

"I took the children out back while I worked in the garden. I needed to do something constructive before I exploded. I didn't think about the spare set of keys we had in my desk drawer. When I heard the car starting, I ran to the driveway, but I was too late to stop her. She screeched out of there, knocking over a neighbor's trash can across the street. Alice was doing the very thing I didn't want her to do and it was all my fault. The last words we exchanged were angry, spiteful ones." He clamped his mouth shut, the hard set of his jaw attesting to the anguish he was re-experiencing.

"You aren't responsible for Alice driving the car. *She* chose to do that. Just as *she* chose to drink in the first place. You can't save someone who doesn't want to be saved."

"I should have been able to do something — anything. I'm a doctor. My wife was ill."

"You did. You supported her for years while she drank. You encouraged her to get help. You stood by her when a lot of people wouldn't have."

"There were times I just wanted out and wished I was someplace else." He cradled his head in his hands. "But I never wanted her to die."

His raspy voice penetrated her own pain. Like her, he was hurting inside. She touched his arm and felt the tensing of his muscles beneath her fingertips. "Of course you didn't."

"Because of my actions, my children don't have a mother."

"That's not true. She was the one making the choices, not you. You need to take to heart your own advice."

He plowed his hands through his hair and shot to his feet. "I need to go. I'll be back later to check on Mark."

His rigid stance conveyed his displeasure

at what she'd said. He wasn't ready to listen to his own advice, Kathleen thought as he strode toward the door and yanked it open. Jared was fighting his own demons, and even in the middle of her own torment, she wished she could help him as he had her.

The hospital chapel was small and dimly lit. Kathleen closed the door and all the sounds in the hallway faded from her ears. She made her way past the three rows of pews to sit on the front one. For a long moment she stared at the simple altar, one bright light illuminating it.

She didn't know where to begin.

The silence in the chapel calmed her. With her eyes shut, she thought back over the past few days. Mark had started his medication. He was seeing the psychiatrist. Jared had given her information about schizophrenia as well as a family support group to attend. Her son was going home today. There was so much she needed to say.

"Lord, thank You for returning my son to me." She opened her eyes and looked again at the altar. "Thank You for being there for him when he needed You. He came home unharmed and for that I will be eternally grateful."

Pausing, she laced her fingers together, not sure how to proceed. Finally she simply said, "I know you have every right to turn Your back on me as I did You after John's death." She paused, clearing her throat. "Please help me to be there for Mark. Give me the strength to deal with his illness."

The serenity in the chapel affected a part of her that she had missed these past eighteen months. For the first time in a long while she felt the hand of God on her shoulder, a reminder of His power.

The door opened and the sound of footsteps nearing filled the silence. Jared slipped in beside her.

"The nurse told me you were here."

She offered him a smile. "I thought it was about time I took your advice and spoke with God."

"Has it helped?"

"Yes." She unfolded her hands and stood. "This past week I've realized I can't do this alone."

Jared rose, only inches from her. "You were never alone, but I'm glad you talked with God. When the Lord is in our lives, anything is possible."

His reassurances suffused her with hope. "I'm beginning to believe that again. For a while I forgot." Kathleen started for the chapel door. "Has the paperwork been completed so Mark can go home?"

"Yes, Dr. Martins just left." Jared stepped to the side to allow her to go first into the hallway.

The sights, sounds and smells of a hospital bombarded her as she left the quiet sanctuary. But the reality didn't wash away the hope welling inside her. She was not alone anymore.

"After you two get settled, I'll be by to see how things are going," Jared said, stopping at the nurse's station.

"If you're busy, we'll be okay. I hate taking any more of your time."

Jared frowned. "I'm not Mark's doctor. I'm visiting as a friend."

"But I feel guilty for all the time you've been spending with us."

A grin replaced the frown. "You can just stop feeling guilty. I wanted to spend time with you and Mark. You both are important to me."

A blush seared her cheeks at the intensity of his words. "Then I'll see you later."

Before she headed for Mark's room, Jared said, "You and Mark can count on me, Kathleen."

As Kathleen pushed open her son's door, she wondered again if Jared was using her son to atone for his wife. Was that the only reason he was involved with them? To prove something to himself?

Jared mounted the steps to Kathleen's front porch, raised his hand to ring the bell and paused. Their conversation earlier that day in the chapel came back to haunt him. He dropped his arm to his side and turned away from the door. He still couldn't believe he'd told her about that last day with Alice. He hadn't told a soul, not even Reverend Jones, who had counseled him after Alice's death. But with Kathleen it had just spilled out as though he had no secrets from her.

When had she become so important to him? Since Tulsa? No, before that. From the first day she'd come into his life, he had wanted to be there for her, to help her with her son, but also to be her friend and — And what?

With everything happening in her life, he knew the last thing she needed was someone interested in her as a woman. And yet, he couldn't deny the feelings that were developing. When she smiled, his whole world lit up. When she touched him, it went further than a physical connection.

The front door swung open to reveal

Kathleen standing in the entrance. "I thought I heard a car pull up. I was just going into the kitchen to fix some dinner. You can talk to me while I work."

"It's after nine and you haven't eaten dinner yet? Is everything all right?"

She moved to the side so he could enter her house. "I know it's late for dinner, but time got away from me. Mark and I were talking for a while. He's sleeping now." She turned toward the back of the house. "I'm not used to my son sleeping so much."

"He's getting used to the medication. That should level off soon."

When Jared stepped into Kathleen's kitchen, an immediate warmth surrounded him. He liked this room of her house best. He could tell she loved to cook and spent a lot of time in the kitchen — as he did in his yard. While she withdrew some ingredients from the refrigerator, he enjoyed watching her move. She had a grace about her that made her motions flow.

"Are you hungry? I can make you a sandwich, too," she said as she closed the pantry door.

"I already had dinner with Hannah and Terry."

"Are you sure you don't want something to eat?"

"Please. Fix whatever you want. I'm fine."

She busied herself at the counter while Jared sat at the table and continued his observation. He wanted to make sure she really was okay. The past month had been so rough on Kathleen. There were a few times he'd wondered if she would fall apart in front of his eyes. But somehow she'd managed to keep herself together. He admired that about her. With Alice, whenever something went wrong, she drank.

As Kathleen prepared her sandwich, Jared noted the confidence that emanated from her. Something has changed, he thought. He remembered the look on her face when he had seen her in the chapel. She had been at peace with herself, as if she had truly found the Lord again. He hoped she continued to turn to the Lord, but he hoped she'd also turn to him when she needed help. He realized he liked being needed by her. Alice had never really needed him, not the way he had wanted.

Kathleen finished making her turkey and Swiss cheese sandwich, added some potato chips and brought it to the table. "How about something to drink?" She went back to the refrigerator and removed a green pitcher.

"Sure. Water. Iced tea. Whatever you have."

Kathleen poured two glasses of iced tea and put one down in front of Jared. She popped a chip into her mouth. "I really shouldn't have these; I eat one and I can't stop until half the bag is gone. Please take some if you want."

"No, I'm full. Mrs. Davis fixed a big dinner for us."

"You know, with all that's happened I haven't had a chance to see Hannah much. How's she doing? I miss our talks."

Grinning, Jared relaxed back in the chair. "She's almost reached her goal of saving enough for the electronic game set."

"That's my girl." Kathleen took a bite of her sandwich, then washed it down with a swallow of tea.

A month before Jared had wondered if he should encourage Hannah and Kathleen's friendship. Now he knew he had been right to let it progress. Even if nothing developed between Kathleen and him, he couldn't deny his daughter Kathleen's influence. "Yeah, that's Hannah all right. When she sets her mind on something it would take an act of Congress to get her to change her course."

"That can be a good thing."

"And it can be a bad thing. My tomboy daughter is turning into a young lady this summer. School will start in a few weeks and I don't even want to think about what that will mean."

"Boys calling her?"

"Every night. But not just boys, also girls. I've had to put a time limit on her calls. I didn't know there was that much to talk about."

Kathleen laughed, thinking back to her own childhood. "You might want to consider getting a second phone line for Hannah and Terry, especially since you're on call some evenings."

"Can't I just forbid her talking to anyone until she's eighteen?"

"Sure. I'd love to see how you get that to work."

He lifted his glass and took a long sip of his drink. "Yeah, I guess that would be kinda hard to enforce."

"Maybe just a tad bit." Kathleen held up her forefinger and thumb with no space between them. "How's Terry doing with his summer jobs?"

"Terry is the complete opposite of Hannah. He lasted one day working and when his friends wanted him to play, he decided that was more important than earning money. And any money he gets goes straight through that big hole in his pocket. It's funny how two siblings can be so different."

"That's Laura and me. Only two years apart in age and yet worlds apart in how we do things."

While Kathleen ate some more of her sandwich, Jared reached over and snatched a couple of potato chips from her plate. "You have a nice family. They've been very supportive these past few weeks."

"Yes, they were here a good part of this afternoon until I made them go home. I want Mark's life to be as normal as possible."

"Then I hope he'll start coming to the youth group again."

Kathleen stared at her near-empty plate, frowning. "I don't know. Teenagers can be awful hard on someone who's a little different."

"I agree, but if I talk with them ahead of time and explain to them about what Mark's going through, I think they'll be a great support system for him. He'll need friends as well as his family."

She shook her head. "Still —"

"What about school next month? Don't you think it would be better if he has a base of friends before he goes to a new high school?"

Kathleen blew out a frustrated breath. "Boy, this isn't easy. You're right. Mark's life hasn't come to a standstill and I can't treat him as if it has. Mark needs to go to school and he'll need friends to help him."

"If not this Sunday then next Sunday, bring him to the meeting."

"Okay." She glanced at Jared and wondered when he had become so important to her. She had no business caring so much what he thought. But she did. She didn't need to get involved with anyone, especially Jared who had been so hurt by his wife. His scars ran deep and she wasn't sure they were healed yet.

"If it's all right with you, I can talk to the kids this week and get everything set up."

"That'll be fine," Kathleen said, feeling as though one chapter in her life had closed and another had opened. Like her son's, her life wasn't stagnant. When Mark was better, she would need to get on with her own life, and suddenly she knew she wanted Jared to be a part of that. That realization both frightened her and intrigued her.

CHAPTER NINE

Jared slipped into the pew beside Kathleen the first Sunday in August. "I thought I'd find you here."

"I wanted to give Mark some space." She scanned her church's sanctuary, the quiet comforting. "This is a good place to think."

"I know what you mean. Everything okay?"

"As well as can be expected. Actually I can't complain. Mark's settling into a routine. I wasn't sure he'd agree to come to the youth group meeting, but he did. His cousin had something to do with that. Shane's been a great support. My whole family has been."

"That's important when dealing with a situation like Mark's."

"I know. The support group I'm attending has helped me learn how to cope and be there for my son. Thank you for putting me in touch with them." She smiled at Jared, wanting to convey in that one gesture how important his friendship was to her.

He returned her smile, trapping her hand in his warm grasp. "You're welcome."

"I came in here to thank God for letting me know what was wrong with Mark. At least now I know what we must do to make things better. Not knowing was tearing me up inside."

"The unknown is scary, but knowing the Lord is with us makes it better."

"I am not alone. Mark is not alone. That's something I've had to learn lately. There for a time I forgot."

Jared squeezed her hand. "It's sometimes hard to remember when we're dealing with a tragedy."

"Is that experience talking? You've had moments of doubt, too?"

He lifted his shoulders in a shrug. "I'm human. The last year with Alice was very trying."

"But you didn't lose faith?"

"Not in God."

"In yourself?"

His chest expanded as he inhaled a deep breath. He exhaled slowly, his eyes veiled with an emotion that was hard to read. "Yes."

The finality in his answer put an end to the discussion. He released her hand, that quickly chilled after the warmth from his touch.

"I assume since you're in here that the meeting is over with."

"Yes. They're eating now and playing games in the rec hall. Too hot to go outside and do anything." Jared rolled his shoulders as though to ease the tension gripping them, but their taut set remained.

Jared rose and held his hand out. "Why don't you come back to the rec hall, have some pizza — which is probably cold by now. Mark is there."

She knew that Jared was making an effort to put what they had been talking about behind him. She also knew that one day he would have to face his problems concerning the death of his wife. As he had been there for her, she wanted to be there for him. She put her hand in his and stood.

"Lead the way. Cold pizza sounds good."

When they entered the recreational hall, Jared headed for the table where the food was spread out. "I should have realized there wouldn't be any pizza left." He looked sheepish. "All I can offer you is pop and cookies."

"I guess I could start with dessert and work my way backward through dinner."

"If we don't hurry, dessert won't even be an option." Jared handed Kathleen a napkin.

Kathleen took a bite of a chocolate chip cookie. "Who made this?"

"Hannah. Mrs. Davis isn't too pleased that Hannah's taken an interest in cooking. My daughter has invaded her domain and I don't think that's gonna change any time soon."

"Tell Hannah these are delicious." She chewed another bite of her cookie.

"Why don't you tell her? You and Mark can come to dinner tomorrow night."

"Are you sure?" Kathleen asked, remembering the last time they had all had dinner together, when Mark had kicked in the television set.

"Yes, we need to make Mark's life as normal as possible. *Your* life needs to be as normal as possible."

Kathleen grinned. "Then I accept. Are you going to cook?"

"No way," Jared said with a chuckle. "That's what I pay Mrs. Davis for."

"It'll be good to see Hannah and Terry again. I didn't get to talk to them at church earlier today."

"Hannah will be excited to hear you're coming to dinner. I won't be surprised if she makes some more cookies."

"I seem to remember I promised her I would take her shopping again before school starts. We'll have to plan an outing."

Jared stepped into her personal space and leaned close to whisper, "Thank you. I wasn't sure how to ask you to do that for me."

His nearness sent her heart beating fast. "You can ask me anything, Jared. After all you've done for me, this is nothing."

"Not to Hannah. You've touched my daughter's life."

How about yours? Kathleen wondered.

Hannah threw open the front door, a huge grin on her face. "I'm so glad you could come over tonight."

Kathleen responded with her own smile, the child's enthusiasm spreading. "I couldn't pass up a home-cooked meal."

The young girl puffed out her chest. "I made dessert. Cookies."

"If they're anything like the ones I had last night, I'm throwing my diet out the window."

"Hannah, are you going to let our guests in or are we going to have dinner out on the front porch?" Jared came up behind his daughter, placing a hand on her shoulder. "I'm glad you could come, Mark."

"Thanks," Kathleen's son mumbled, looking uncomfortable, his eyes downcast.

"Mark, you are always welcome here." Jared closed the door and gestured for everyone to go into the den off to the left.

"Where's Terry?" Kathleen surveyed the large room with its overstuffed furniture and paneled walls that shone with a rich walnut luster. She could tell the family spent many nights in the den. There was a reading corner, a desk with a computer on it, a game table and a big television set.

"He went upstairs to get a game for us to play later."

Just as Jared finished explaining, Terry ran into the room with a box clutched in his hands. "I found it."

"Good. We'll play after we eat."

"Play what?" Kathleen asked, trying to see what Terry put on the game table.

"Clue," Hannah said, pulling Kathleen over to the table to show her the box. "This is Dad's favorite game."

Kathleen peered at Jared. "You like a good murder?"

"Oh, yes. You ought to see what I read in between the medical journals."

"Why, Dr. Matthews, I am surprised. You're a healer."

"Who enjoys a good book that gets my old heart thumping."

"I never considered reading an aerobic

exercise. That's one I might consider doing."

Kathleen watched Mark prowl the room, checking out the computer before walking toward the TV. She tensed even though the set wasn't turned on. When her son passed the television and went to the bookshelves next to it, she released a breath she hadn't even realized she was holding.

Jared leaned close and murmured, "He'll be fine. He's taken his medication. He seems much calmer each time I see him, more attuned to his surroundings. Remember that last night he joined in with the group he was sitting with."

"I know. But the fear is there. What if he has another psychotic episode?"

"You'll handle it like the first one."

Kathleen started to say that she hoped so, that she prayed every day for the strength to deal with Mark, but Terry interrupted with, "Dad, I'm hungry. When are we gonna eat?"

Jared glanced at his son. "Right now."

As Terry hurried from the room, Kathleen noticed he kept his distance from her son. She couldn't blame the boy for being wary of Mark. Even her son saw the look Terry gave him and frowned. He hung back, motioning to Kathleen to stay, while

Hannah and Jared left the den.

"I'm not that hungry. I'd rather stay in here."

"Why, Mark?"

Her son stared down at the floor, his brow creased. "Dr. Martins and I talked about what I did. I think Terry is scared of me."

Kathleen put her arm around his shoulder and was glad when her son didn't flinch. "Then come into the dining room and show him things have changed. That you're better."

He sighed. "I guess I can do that."

Kathleen walked with her son toward the dining room. Maybe they shouldn't have come tonight. Was she expecting too much of Mark? Was she letting her growing feelings for Jared color her perception?

There were two places left for her and Mark when they entered the room. One was at the end of the table and the other on the side across from Hannah and Terry. When Kathleen sat facing Jared and scanned the table, for a brief moment she felt as if they were a family. The realization they weren't brought a dull ache to her heart. She had always wanted more children and that didn't seem possible. She had to think of Mark first and foremost, and how could she ask someone else to take on the burden of caring for her son? Even someone as wonderful as Jared had his limitations.

The aroma of onions and other spices mingled with freshly baked bread. When Mrs. Davis came out of the kitchen and put two large pizzas on the table, Mark's eyes gleamed. Kathleen sent a warm smile to Jared. Pizza was her son's favorite food and even though it had been served the evening before, it was a perfect choice for three children.

Terry started to reach for a piece when Jared said, "Let's give thanks first, son."

Terry snatched his hand back and dropped his head while Jared said, "Lord, thank You for all this wonderful food but most especially for the company of good friends. Watch over all at this table tonight and be always in our lives. Amen."

Terry mumbled amen quickly, then grabbed two pieces of pepperoni pizza with everything on it. Hannah followed suit with Mark right behind her.

"School starts soon," Kathleen said, all the children groaning. "I thought if you wanted, Hannah, I could take you shopping again for clothes."

"Really?" Hannah's eyes grew round. "Are you sure?"

Kathleen nodded. "I could use some new

clothes myself and wouldn't mind your input."

"You mean it? You want my help?"

"Yes, we could do it some time this week."

"How about me?" Terry asked, gulping down a huge swallow of milk that left a white mustache on his face.

"I've got to take Mark shopping for school. Why don't you come along then if that's okay with your dad?"

"Sure." Jared's eyes crinkled at the corners, his two dimples appearing.

Terry looked down at his plate and didn't say a word. Tension swept through the room, chilling the air.

Mark shifted in his chair, scooted it back and rose. "Excuse me."

The minute her son left, Hannah rounded on Terry. "I'll go with Kathleen and Mark shopping. I'm no scaredy-cat."

"Hannah!"

Jared's stern voice sliced through the mounting tension. Terry's hunched shoulders and downcast eyes made Kathleen's heart wrench.

She stood and walked to his chair, squatting down next to it and touching the young boy's arm. "Terry, I understand why you are afraid of my son. I would be glad to take you shopping alone. Just you and me and afterward we can visit the ice-cream store. There's a hot caramel sundae with my name on it, just waiting for me to walk through the door."

With eyes glistening, Terry glanced at her. "You don't mind going three times?"

"No. My son has been helping his grandparents in their backyard. It'll give him more time to be with them." Kathleen didn't say that she didn't leave Mark alone, not yet. Even though he was sixteen, she was afraid she would return home and find him gone again. The memories of searching for him were still too fresh in her mind.

"It's Colonel Mustard in the kitchen with a knife," Jared announced triumphantly to everyone sitting at the game table.

Hannah and Terry groaned. Kathleen handed Jared the pack to check his answer. He slipped the three cards out and smiled.

"You always win," Hannah said with a pout.

"Can we play again? That was what I was going to say my next turn." Mark tore off his paper and crumbled it in his hand, tossing it on the table next to him.

"Sure. If everyone else wants to play again." Jared shuffled the cards.

Kathleen checked her watch. "We have time for one more game."

"Can I be red this time?" Terry asked Mark.

Mark slid the game piece to Terry.

While Jared dealt the cards to each player, he thought about the past hour playing with Kathleen, Mark and his children. This was the way a family should be, he mused as he looked at his cards and marked his paper. Even Terry was relaxed now around Mark. And Mark had gotten into the game, winning the first one. The smile that had graced the teenager's face had lit the whole room. But best of all was Kathleen's accompanying look of happiness.

He knew in his marriage to Alice there had been times like this, but as the years passed they had become fewer and fewer. Kathleen was the kind of mother he wanted his children to have, but could he risk his heart again to give his children what they needed?

Terry went first. "Look out. Here I come. I'm gonna win this one. Red's my favorite color."

"If that's the case then I'll win. Yellow's my favorite color." Hannah took the dice and threw it. When she got a two, her face fell.

"Better luck next time, squirt." Mark took his turn, moving his game piece six spaces into a room.

Jared caught Kathleen's gaze across the table. A light shone in her eyes that touched a part of him he thought had died a long time ago. He began to dream — dream of a family, whole and complete with a mother and a father for his children. The vision began to grow as each player took another turn.

When Jared started to pick up the dice for the third time, the phone rang. "Hold everything. I'll be right back." He hurried to the desk and snatched up the receiver. "Hello."

Kathleen watched Jared's happy expression melt into a frown, his brow deeply furrowed. She knew something was wrong. All her attention focused on Jared as he finished his conversation and put the phone back on its hook. He pivoted.

"There's been an emergency with one of my patients. He's at the hospital and Mrs. Davis is gone for the evening."

"Mark and I will stay here until you return."

"I can't —" Jared looked at Kathleen, his taut shoulders relaxing. "Thanks. I appreciate the help. I don't know how long I'll be."

"That's okay. If Mark gets tired, he can sleep on the couch. When do Hannah and Terry need to be in bed?"

Jared headed across the room toward the door. "Terry by nine-thirty. Hannah ten-thirty."

Kathleen noticed Hannah sticking her tongue out at Terry and the young boy returning the gesture. "We'll finish the game without you. We'll disperse your cards among us."

At the door Jared paused. "I don't need to tell you two to mind Kathleen, do I?" He pointedly looked from Terry to Hannah.

They both shook their heads.

"Can we have ice cream before we go to bed?" Terry asked, grabbing the dice to toss.

"That's fine." Jared left the den.

"Now I know I'm gonna win," Mark said, taking his turn and moving five spaces.

By the time the game ended twenty minutes later Hannah had managed to win and taunted her little brother with that fact.

"Losers get to clean up," Hannah announced, sitting back in her chair and folding her arms over her chest.

"Oh, no, Hannah. You have it backward. The winner gets the privilege of cleaning up while the rest of us get our ice cream."

Kathleen rose, biting her bottom lip to keep a straight face.

"I don't get any ice cream?"

"You do as soon as this mess is cleaned up. We'll be in the kitchen."

"But —" hung in the air as Kathleen hurried the boys from the room.

In the kitchen she filled four bowls with chocolate chip ice cream. As Terry and Mark sat down at the table, Hannah came bounding into the room, her face flushed from rushing. She spied her bowl and quickly grabbed it, then flopped into a chair next to her brother.

Kathleen joined the group. "After you finish your ice cream, Terry, you'll need to get ready for bed."

"It's still early. It's only —" the young boy spied the clock on the wall, his mouth curving downward.

"Boy, the time sure does fly when you're having fun. It's nine-fifteen already. Time for little boys to go to bed," Hannah said with a huge grin. She scooped up a large spoonful of ice cream and popped it into her mouth.

Terry started to protest. Kathleen held up her hand. "Hannah."

The young girl stared at her bowl and mumbled an apology. Terry beamed, finishing his last bite.

★ ★ ★

Jared let himself into his house, the quiet a balm after the hectic few hours at the hospital. "Home," he sighed the word as he walked down the hall toward the light in the den.

When he entered the room, he found Kathleen asleep in the lounge chair, her head cocked to the side, her feet propped up, her face relaxed. Beautiful. His heart expanded at the sight of her in his house as though she belonged here forever. That thought sent a jolt through him.

Moving further into the den, Jared noticed Mark asleep on the couch, one arm dangling over the edge. If he checked, he knew his children would be in bed upstairs. Again the feeling that Kathleen belonged in his life inundated him.

Quietly he made his way to the chair and knelt down beside it. He hated to wake her up, but it was after midnight. He watched her for a few minutes, the gentle rise and fall of her chest, the serene cast to her features, as though she had not a trouble in the world. He wanted that for her and would do everything in his power to make that true.

Slowly, almost hesitantly, he brought his hand up to touch her arm to wake her up. "Kathleen."

Her eyes slid open and she stared at him, her lids half closed. A smile leisurely graced her mouth, then her eyes. She stirred, straightening. "What time is it?"

"Nearly one."

"How's your patient? Everything okay?" She put the leg rest down and brought the chair up.

Jared rose, hovering over her. "He'll be fine in a few days. Nothing too serious."

"Good." Kathleen combed her fingers through her hair and swallowed several times to coat her dry throat. "I must have been more tired than I thought. I didn't mean to fall asleep." She searched the room until she saw Mark sleeping on the couch. The tension in her shoulders eased. "We'd better go home."

"How would you like to go sailing next weekend?" He hadn't meant to blurt the invitation out like that, but one look at her beautiful face, her hair disheveled, and he couldn't help himself.

"Sailing?"

"I keep a sailboat at the lake." He offered her his hand and helped her up. "I want to make it clear it would be just you and me. No kids."

"A date?"

"Yes," he murmured, realizing he still

211

held her hand between them, only inches separating them. "I'm asking you out on our first official date. What do you say? We can have lunch and go sailing."

"I didn't know you had a sailboat."

"There are a lot of things you probably don't know about me and I'm sure there are a lot of things I don't know about you. But I want to know." He shifted even closer. "I want to know everything."

She gulped, her eyes widening. "You do?"

"Kathleen, I'm not going to fight this attraction between us anymore. I want to see where it will take us."

"Yes."

"Yes, you'll go?" His heartbeat accelerated.

She nodded, her eyes a soft brown. "How can I turn down an invitation like that? I've never been sailing and the idea sounds intriguing. But most of all, I want to spend time with you."

He framed her face with his hands and brought his mouth down on hers. The touching of their lips sent his heart racing even more. His fingers delved into the short strands of her hair, the feel silky. Her scent of lilacs washed over him.

When they parted, he felt as though he'd lost something. He wanted to kiss her again and again, but with Kathleen he would have to take things slow and easy or he would frighten her. For his own sake, he needed to take things slow and easy. His bruised emotions were still too raw not to be cautious.

CHAPTER TEN

The sun bathed Kathleen with warmth while the wind caressed her skin with coolness. The sound of the sails flapping in the breeze mingled with the lapping of the water against the boat. Not a cloud in the sky and the lake was smooth, calm. A perfect day, she thought as she lifted her face to the sun.

"I was worried when the weatherman said we had a fifty-fifty chance of rain today." Jared sat behind the wheel on the thirty-foot sailboat, dressed in jean shorts, a white T-shirt and deck shoes.

"Is this the same weatherman from church that you listen to every morning? The one who predicts rain when there isn't a cloud for a hundred miles?"

"You need to stop listening to Hannah," Jared grumbled with an exaggerated frown.

"On the contrary. She has some wonderful stories to tell."

"I'm afraid even to ask what she has been saying."

"Nothing too damaging." Closing her

eyes, she pretended to settle back as though she was going to sunbathe and not elaborate.

She felt Jared's presence towering over her. Her eyes snapped open. "Who's driving the boat?"

He smiled. "No one. What did she say?"

"I'll tell you if you go back over there and put your hands on the wheel."

He backed away, his hands up in the air. "Okay. If you insist on me steering this boat, I will, but I want to know what stories my daughter has been telling you."

"Fine." Kathleen swung her legs around to face him. "Your daughter is a fountain of information."

"That's what I'm afraid of." He slipped behind the wheel, his whole attention riveted to her. "Spill it. What did she tell you?"

She shrugged. "Nothing really."

"Kathleen Somers, I can't believe you said that after telling me my daughter is a gossip."

"I didn't say that."

"Okay. A fountain of information. The same thing."

"No, it isn't. Information and gossip are two different things."

He rose, a menacing expression on his

face. "Do you want me to come over there and —"

Laughing, Kathleen shook her head. "I'll tell. You stay put." She crossed her legs and lounged back against the seat cushion. "Really it wasn't anything. I just wanted to know what else you might have — like a sailboat — that you'd neglected to tell me about." Picking up her white hat, she put it on to shield her face. "I was afraid you would want me to go flying in a plane or something like that."

"What's wrong with flying in a plane?"

"I'm one of those people who feel if we were meant to fly we would have wings like birds."

"Rest assured, I have no plane tucked away."

"Yes, I know."

"What else do you know?"

His penetrating gaze seized hers. The intensity of his look captured her words and held them. Finally she blinked, breaking the visual connection. "I know if I don't put more sunscreen on, I'll be a painful shade of red by the end of the day."

"Kathleen."

The warning in his voice quivered down her. "Hannah really didn't say much."

"Don't forget I know my daughter well.

She loves to talk."

"I know you don't have a plane. She did tell me about the cabin you all have rented every July for two weeks. Why didn't you do that this year?"

Jared looked away.

"Was it because of Mark?"

"We were kind of busy. Before I knew it, July was over. Now it's August and school starts in a week. It's no big deal."

She rose, making her way to where he was and sat beside him. "It is a big deal to me."

"Was Hannah upset?"

"No. She's too busy earning money, but I think Terry is disappointed you all didn't go this summer."

"I'll talk with him. I thought I explained. I told him we would go later — maybe spring break."

"Oh, you did. But that doesn't mean he was happy with the change in plans."

"He should have said something. Hannah should have said something."

"I think your children are trying to protect you."

His hands on the wheel tightened, his knuckles white. "Protect me? Why do they think I need protecting?"

Kathleen laced her fingers together and stared at her hands. "Remember they were living in the same household as you were when Alice was drinking. Hannah knows you weren't happy."

"But I tried to keep that from them."

"Hannah is a smart young girl. She worries about you."

"She told you all this when you two were shopping?"

"Some. I'm glad she feels she can confide in me."

"Why didn't she say anything to me?"

The tone in his voice spoke of his hurt and Kathleen wanted to soothe it as he had hers so many times. "Because sometimes it is easier to talk to an outsider."

He covered her clasped hands. "Kathleen, I don't think Hannah thinks of you as an outsider and I think that's the reason she has talked to you. Thank you for being there for her."

The warmth of his palm against her skin sent her pulse hammering through her veins. "I love helping her."

"I know. I'm finding that's the kind of person you are."

"I miss volunteering. I used to do a lot in Shreveport."

"Well, Mrs. Somers, then I've got a deal for you."

She responded to his light tone with a

laugh. "An offer I can't refuse?"

"Yep. Volunteering. Working with people. Seeing me from time to time."

"You're right. How can I refuse that?"

"You can't."

"Since we've established I can't refuse the opportunity, care to tell me what it is?"

"Remember when I told you about needing a volunteer coordinator at the hospital? We still need one. How about doing it when Mark starts school? It'll give you something to do that you love."

"You're right. It's an offer I can't refuse. I'd like to if everything with Mark keeps going as it is. I'm starting to leave him by himself for short periods of time, but I'd like him to be in school before I devote myself to the volunteer coordinator's position."

"Where is he today? At home?"

"No. He's at Laura's." She slanted a look at Jared. "Who was more than eager to have him since I was going out on my first official date in years."

Jared's chuckle was low. "That sounds like Laura."

"I'm surprised your ears weren't burning this morning. She had to give me advice on what to do on a date. She thinks I'm date-challenged since I haven't dated anyone in years and the only guy I ever dated seriously was my husband."

His chuckle evolved into a robust laugh. "I'm afraid to ask what her advice was."

"She gave me a list of topics to keep the conversation going."

"We don't seem to have a problem there."

Jared still held her hand, reminding her it was more than a first date. They had come a long way together over the past few months. "No, we have a lot in common."

He rubbed his thumb across the back of her hand. "Two single parents trying to raise their children the best way they can."

"That sums us up nicely."

"Anything else Laura said?"

His thumb continued to massage her hand, going back and forth over her knuckles. The action brought a weakness to her limbs. "Under no circumstances was I to let you kiss me on our first date. A kiss isn't allowed until the third date."

"I think we've gone beyond that."

Kathleen remembered the kiss he had given her in his den the week before. Yes, definitely beyond their first kiss. She had wanted so much more in those few minutes he'd held her, his large hands cupping her face. Those feelings had surprised her and frightened her. The only man she'd ever wanted to be with was her husband and now she was thinking about — She shook those thoughts from her mind. Too much. Too fast. She was still trying to piece her life together.

"Laura takes her role of big sis very seriously," Kathleen murmured, gently tugging her hand from his grasp. She needed space before she forgot her sister's sage advice. She needed to slow things down. She scooted back on the cushion and twisted her body so she could face him on the bench.

"You have a wonderful, supportive family. That's important."

"Yes, especially now. They have been there for Mark from the beginning. Like you." Kathleen brought her legs up and hugged them to her. "I thank God every day for the people around me."

"It's good to hear you talk about the Lord like that."

"That's another thing I have you to thank for. You made me realize I should be turning to God in my troubled times, not away. Your own experience with Alice and how you dealt with that has only reinforced what I needed to do. Because there are no instant solutions, I blamed the Lord for my problems. I'd forgotten how important patience was, and just listening. Now every day I begin by praying and I end by praying. It helps me to put my day in perspective."

"Here, keep your hands on the wheel while I change course."

Kathleen scrambled forward as Jared stood, releasing the wheel. Making his way to the front, Jared busied himself with bringing one sail down. After securing it, he came back to where she sat.

"You're doing great, Kathleen. I'll make a sailor out of you yet."

"That's okay. You can have the wheel back. We're heading for that island and I don't want us to run aground."

He slipped in beside her and she moved away, putting several feet between them.

"I thought we would have lunch on the island and do some exploring."

"I haven't been to Sunset Cove since I was a child. Is there still a dock there?"

"Yes. In need of repair but usable."

"Good. I really didn't want to wade in to the island."

"Kathleen, where's your sense of adventure?"

"When I'm on an adventure, I still like creature comforts. If I remember correctly, there's a lot of sand on the beaches. As a child I didn't mind wearing half the beach on me. As an adult I do."

"This from a woman who would go into the bayous."

"Yes, but I was in a boat, not walking or wading."

Jared maneuvered the sailboat alongside the dock and Kathleen jumped off the boat to tie the ropes to the wooden poles. As she finished, she stepped back and her foot went through a hole in the pier where the wood had rotted. She pulled on her foot to free it and nearly toppled to the planks. She caught herself and managed to pry her tennis shoe from the hole.

Jared leaped off the boat and was at her side instantly. "Are you hurt?"

Heat scorched her cheeks. "No, just embarrassed that after only a minute on the island, I get into trouble."

"Some of us have been talking about fixing this pier. This clinches it for me. It's getting too dangerous to use. We can eat our lunch on the boat, then leave."

"No. I want to see Sunset Cove. We're here. We'll just be careful as we make our way to shore. Besides, I have my very own doctor if anything else goes wrong."

After Jared retrieved the food hamper and a blanket, Kathleen followed him from the pier, walking where he did. On the small beach she scanned the area, the scent of water and vegetation permeating the warm air. A crow cawed in the distance while a white tern flew overhead, shrieking. No one else was on the island. The isolation, as though they were cut off from civilization, whisked her worries away. There was only this moment in time, Kathleen thought as she slowly turned, remembering outings as a child when she and Laura had played make-believe games about damsels in distress and pirates. So much had happened since then. She had loved and lost. Was it possible for love to come a second time around? The kind of love that connected two people on all levels? For having had it once had spoiled her for any kind of love except that.

"Where would you like to eat lunch?" Jared asked, coming up behind her.

"Is there still a stream on the other side that empties into the lake?"

"Yes."

"Then how about there?"

"Fine. Do you want to go around by the beach or through the woods?"

"Through the woods. There should be a path to the other side."

When Kathleen entered the grove of oaks, pines and maple trees that graced the middle of the small island, the coolness of the woods chased away the heat of the day. Streams of sunlight flowed from the upper reaches of the trees to illuminate the path. As they walked toward the other side of the island, the crunch of pine needles and leaves cut into the silence of the forest.

Kathleen heard the stream before she saw it. Emerging from thick underbrush, she took in the water bubbling over the rocks toward the lake.

"Nothing's changed. We can spread our blanket out near the water's edge," Kathleen said, walking ahead of Jared to the spot.

He helped her to smooth the blanket over the ground, then he opened the basket. "Mrs. Davis prepared everything except the cookies. Hannah insisted on baking us some."

"She said something about it when we went shopping."

"You two must talk the whole time you're gone."

"Something like that," Kathleen began opening containers to reveal fried chicken, coleslaw and potato salad.

"I miss her talking to me. But at her age there are things she doesn't want to say to a man, even her father."

"The same thing happened to me when

Mark got to a certain age. Mark and John were very close."

"Terry has mentioned several times about the shopping trip coming up with Mark."

"I was worried he wouldn't want to go because of Mark's behavior that night at Laura's. I'm glad he changed his mind."

"We talked about that. He thought Mark had been drinking and that was why he kicked in the TV screen."

Kathleen stopped scooping out coleslaw onto the paper plates. "Drinking? Why?"

"Because right before Alice died, she started throwing things and breaking them when she was angry, which was a lot at the end. Terry remembers."

Her throat constricted around the words she wanted to say. Jared's pain was always there just under the surface, ready to reveal itself on a moment's notice.

"I explained again that Mark wasn't able to control his actions. He seemed to accept that, but he asked about his mother and why she did those things."

She placed her hand over her heart as though that would stop its quick thumping. "What did you say?"

"That his mother couldn't control her behavior, either. That she had an illness that made her do things she normally wouldn't have."

Kathleen finished dishing up the food, her hands trembling as she held the plates. Even though Mark and Alice had two different illnesses, the effect on the family was similar. Again she wondered if Jared was trying to atone for his wife through her son. She knew that wasn't really possible. What would happen when Jared realized that?

"For a small hospital it's well equipped." Kathleen stepped onto the elevator and punched the down button.

Jared leaned back against the wall. "We're quite proud of the facility, especially since it serves the smaller communities in the surrounding area as well as Crystal Springs."

No one else was on the elevator, and she felt as though they were in their own small world, the atmosphere charged. "So many rural areas lack hospitals and even doctors."

He laughed. "I wouldn't call Crystal Springs rural, exactly. It has thirty-five thousand people."

"You would think you were born here."

"Transplanted but perfectly content with the town."

"Don't you mean bustling metropolis?" His very presence heightened her senses.

His scent teased her nostrils. His casual attire of tan slacks and white golf shirt underscored his relaxed aura, making her aware of how Jared was at home in many different environments.

"Next you're going to swear you saw Superman flying over." The doors swished open and he signaled that she exit first. "I do believe, Mrs. Somers, you're making fun of me."

She smiled back at him, enjoying the repartee. "Only with the best intentions." Stopping halfway down the corridor, she faced Jared. Their gazes connected, forming an instant bond between them, which was happening a lot lately. Suddenly her mouth went dry. "You said something about an office with a view of the garden," she finally murmured, her words raspy as though she wasn't used to talking.

He severed eye contact, the moment of connection evaporating. "There's an office next to mine that's vacant. Since I'm head of pediatrics, which doesn't mean a whole lot since there are only five pediatricians in Crystal Springs, I spend probably half my time here and the other half at my office on Fifth Street." He thrust open a door and stepped aside. "What do you think?"

Kathleen moved past Jared into the small

room. "A desk, a phone, a file cabinet and a window. What more could a gal ask for?"

"I know you can barely turn around in here, but it's private and quiet."

"You're fattening the deal with each word you speak. Will I get a chair?"

The lines at the corners of his eyes crinkled while merriment danced in his expression. "I thought you could use the desk for that."

"I suppose I could. It would give me more room to move around in here if I didn't have a chair," she said in a deadly serious voice. She hopped up onto the wooden top, crossing her legs and leaning back, her arms propping her up.

His gaze trekked from her head to her toes. "I'll make sure there's a chair here by this afternoon."

His laughter was rich and full. Kathleen responded to it, a warmth suffusing her face at the interest she saw in his expression. "Such service. I'm impressed."

"Anything to get you to stay. I'm just glad I could con — I mean, persuade you to take the position, especially since it's unpaid."

"But I like the hours." Sliding off the desk, Kathleen walked to the window and peered at the garden below. Numerous colors — from pinks to yellows to blues —

greeted her inspection. The sun-drenched trees swayed in the breeze. A cardinal flew from a branch to the ground, bright red against a sea of green. "And you can't beat this view."

Jared came up behind her. She shivered even though the sun cloaked her. Again his spicy lime scent engulfed her, seemingly shrinking the size of the room even more.

"I can't argue with you. I enjoy looking out my window when I have a moment to rest."

She twisted about slightly, his face only inches from hers. She coated her still dry throat and said, "Rest? You're allowed to rest?"

"Not much with school starting. Everyone forgets to the last minute about the shots their children need, not to mention all the supplies Hannah and Terry need. I have to thank you again for taking them to get their school clothes. That was a big help."

She flattened her back against the windowpane, his nearness unraveling her composure. "I'm just returning the favor. Mark's in school today partly because of you."

He leaned into her, eroding what little space was between them. "I'm glad we could help each other out."

The husky appeal in his voice melted her insides. She gripped the window ledge to keep herself upright. He brushed his finger along her jawline, the caress feather-soft. His eyes darkened, his attention completely centered on her. In that moment she felt very special and totally feminine. Slowly he lowered his head toward her and whispered his lips across hers. Her fingernails dug into the wooden ledge.

"I hope we continue to help each other out," he murmured, right before kissing her.

Lost in the wonderful sensations his kiss produced, Kathleen sagged against him. He gripped her shoulders and held her pressed to him. An eternity later, he released her and moved back.

With their gazes bound, she took a deep, composing breath, blowing it out slowly. This was their second kiss and she felt as weak-kneed as she had after the first one. He was the only man other than her husband who had kissed her in years. And, as before, she was totally unprepared for it and the effect it had on her.

"Thank you for showing me the hospital and my very own office," she finally said, needing to fill the silence that hung between them. "I guess this is official now. I am the new volunteer coordinator for the hospital. Even if I'm not getting paid, the title sounds impressive."

"You are my first choice."

"I am your only choice."

"True, but that doesn't change that I feel you will be great at the job."

She blushed, the heat spreading rapidly through her. She never could handle compliments well. "I hardly slept last night because I was thinking about what I could do as the volunteer coordinator."

"I knew I liked you for a good reason. You're quite the dynamo."

"Just doing my job."

Jared glanced at his watch. "I have some time before my first appointment today. Would you like something to eat or maybe a cup of coffee?"

"From the vending machine off the lobby?"

"I have to be pretty desperate to drink that — stuff. I can't even call it coffee. No, I was thinking of Bill's Diner across the street."

"Oh, good. There for a second I thought you had gone over the edge." She shoved away from the window, glad that her legs could support her.

Outside, Kathleen lifted her face to the

sun and relished the warmth on her skin after the coldness of the air-conditioned building. "Before long, autumn will be here."

"My favorite time of year."

"When everything is vibrant," she said as they crossed the street. "This little corner of Arkansas is gorgeous in the fall."

Inside the café Jared wove his way toward a back booth and sat. He waved toward some customers several tables over.

The waitress filled Jared's cup with coffee and asked, "The usual, Doc?"

"Yes," he answered, then said to Kathleen, "The doughnuts are wonderful. They melt in your mouth."

"No, just a cup of hot tea please." After the waitress left, Kathleen added, "When we visited here, this is one of the first places we would come. Mark loves the doughnuts, too." She frowned. "I should have realized something was terribly wrong when we moved here, and Mark didn't say a word about coming to Bill's Diner for doughnuts. You know, when you look back on the situation, there were clues all over the place."

"When we're living through a difficult situation, things aren't that clear. Looking back is always much clearer."

The waitress brought Kathleen her tea

and Jared his doughnuts, then refreshed his coffee.

Jared bit into his glazed doughnut. "Sure you don't want one? They're delicious."

"If I took a bite, I'd gain ten pounds. Just watching you, I'm sure I've put on a pound or two."

The gleam in his blue eyes dimmed with concern. "I can have the waitress take these away if it bothers you I'm eating them."

Laughing, Kathleen shook her head. "Better you than me. I don't begrudge anyone who can manage to eat two glazed doughnuts and not show it." Involuntarily her gaze traveled over the portion of his body showing above the table. There wasn't an ounce of fat on the man. "Do you make a regular habit of eating these?"

"Once a week I indulge. I figure I owe myself a treat."

"You believe in pampering yourself?"

He grinned. "I wouldn't put it quite that way."

"Guys should pamper themselves, too."

His grin broadened, his two dimples readily appearing. "Getting a treat sounds more —" He searched for a word.

"Manly?"

"I was going to say appropriate."

"Sure you were." Kathleen lifted her mug

and sipped, watching him as he took another bite of the first doughnut. Her mouth watered. She licked her lips as though that action would satisfy her craving for sugar. She worked hard to keep her weight where it should be. Desperate to take her mind off what Jared was eating, she said, "While I was tossing and turning last night, I came up with an idea for recruiting volunteers. I'd like to approach the youth group at church and see if they would be interested in working at the hospital."

"Like candy stripers?"

"Sort of, but I want boys and girls to be involved. If I can get your group interested, then I will go to other youth groups in Crystal Springs. There is a wealth of talent in teenagers that I could tap into. I would like to put it to good use."

Jared finished up his first doughnut, washing it down with a swallow of coffee. "I like it. The kids in the youth group have done things at the hospital before at Christmas. They enjoyed themselves."

"I'd like them to be particularly involved with the children and older patients, especially the ones who don't have a lot of family." Kathleen poured some more hot water into her cup and dunked another tea bag in it, trying not to watch Jared eat his second doughnut. Her stomach rumbled and she ignored it. "I hope I can get Mark interested in playing for the patients. He still has his old guitar that he first learned to play on. I want to get him involved in his music again. I think that will help him."

"Why not come to the meeting next Sunday night and put your idea before the group?"

"I'll come as long as you don't rope me into playing any sports."

"Good. I'll pick you and Mark up. After the meeting, I'll get Hannah and Terry and we can go out to dinner."

Like a family, Kathleen thought instantly. She dumped a packet of sugar into her tea and stirred it. But how could she ever ask someone else to share the burden of Mark's illness? Especially someone who had already dealt with a chronic problem?

"Maybe you can get Hannah to tell you about this new boy who's been calling every night since school started."

"Do I hear desperation in your voice?" she asked, pushing the nagging questions to the back of her mind. She and Jared had only had one official date. Blending their two families was a long way off.

"I knew the last boy who called, but this kid is new to Crystal Springs. All Hannah's told me is he moved here last month and all the girls are flipping over him. She has been floating around the house with a silly grin on her face for the past week." Jared took the last bite of his doughnut, then wiped his mouth with his napkin.

His action drew her attention to his lips curved in a half smile. Her gaze slowly rose until it captured his in a visual snare. A long moment passed with nothing said until someone behind Kathleen dropped a plate, its shattering sound reverberating through the diner. She blinked and looked away.

"This summer my daughter has changed from a tomboy into a young lady, and some of that is because of you."

"I'm glad you're saying that with a smile."

"Hannah is happier so I'm happier. You are a good influence on her, Kathleen Somers."

His daughter fulfilled a need in her that was hard to deny. Lately she had been doing a lot of thinking. Always before, with John, her life had revolved around him and Mark. Now she was being forced to define who she really was. One thing she knew was, despite what happened to Mark, she loved being a mother and wished she had more children. Were Hannah and Terry what drew her to Jared? Or was it something much deeper than that?

CHAPTER ELEVEN

"I need some more oregano, Hannah. Can you get it for me?" Kathleen asked as she stirred the pot of spaghetti sauce on her stove. When the phone rang, Kathleen finished with, "Measure out half a teaspoon and add it to the sauce," then hurried to answer the call.

"We're leaving the church. I'll pick up Terry and we'll be over. What are you two fixing for dinner?"

Jared's deep voice quickened her pulse. "Spaghetti." She stared out the window at the darkness that descended so much earlier now that it was the end of September.

"One of my favorites."

"You've said that about everything I've fixed." The compliment sent a warm glow through her.

"I'm finding I have a lot of favorites. See you in a little while."

"Was that Dad?" Hannah carefully filled the measuring spoon with the spice, then dumped it into the large pot.

"He and Mark are going to pick up Terry. They'll be here soon."

A loud rumble of thunder shook the house. Hannah gasped and flinched, dropping the wooden spoon. "I wish it would stop raining."

"Surely these storms won't last much longer."

A flash of lightning followed immediately by a crash of thunder caused the lights to flicker. The frightened look on Hannah's face prompted Kathleen to say, "I have lots of candles if we lose our electricity. Why don't you get some out just in case? They're in that cabinet over there." She gestured toward the last one.

"What about dinner?"

"It's almost done. It might be nice to eat our meal by candlelight. Then after dinner we could tell stories."

"Scary ones?"

"I was thinking more along the line of funny things that have happened to us."

The tension in Hannah's face smoothed away. She withdrew several big, fat candles from the cabinet as well as a box of matches. "I like that idea. I'm not big on scary stories."

"Tell you a secret. Neither am I."

"The guys will probably want to tell scary ones."

Kathleen put the loaf of French bread into the oven, hoping the electricity stayed on long enough to bake it. "We won't give them a choice."

Thunder sounded again. Kathleen saw the fear take hold of Hannah, her eyes wide, her body stiff. "Tell me about what's happening at school. It won't be long before the first nine weeks is over. This year is flying by."

Hannah returned to setting the table. "Jeremy asked me to the fall dance next month."

"Did you say yes?"

Hannah nodded, folding the napkins and placing them by the plates. "I haven't said anything to Dad yet. I'm waiting for the right time."

"Don't wait too long."

"Will you talk to him for me?"

"I could say something to him, but I think you should ask him. He likes Jeremy."

"He told you that?"

"Yes, last week at church when you were talking to Jeremy after the service, he mentioned what a nice boy he was. What happened to the new kid at school?"

A frown darkened Hannah's features. "I found out he was calling a lot of girls. He asked Mary Lou to the dance."

"Does that bother you?"

Hannah shrugged. "At first. Not now. I like Jeremy. He's nicer."

Kathleen heard the front door opening as lightning struck close by. Hannah's face went white. She moved closer to Kathleen. Thunder boomed, rattling the house. The young girl stepped even closer to Kathleen.

"I think we arrived just in time," Jared said, coming into the kitchen with Mark and Terry following close behind him.

Water dripped off all three of them, their hair wet. Kathleen went into the laundry room and retrieved some towels. She handed one to each of the guys. "Have you all heard of rain gear or umbrellas?"

"I don't know if it would have helped. The wind is really picking up out there." Jared took one look at Hannah and added, "But we'll be fine in here." He inhaled a deep breath. "It sure smells wonderful. I'm starved." He headed to the stove to peep into the pot.

"Me, too," Terry said, drying his hair with a towel.

Mark didn't say anything, but he shrugged out of his windbreaker and hung it up on the hook by the back door.

"Go wash up. Dinner should be about ready when you get back." Kathleen filled three glasses with milk and two with iced tea.

While Hannah set the glasses on the table, Kathleen checked the bread, a blast of heat hitting her face when she opened the oven door. The wonderful aroma of food intensified with the scent of baking bread permeating the room. As the guys filed back into the kitchen, Kathleen drained the spaghetti into the colander in the sink.

"Get your plates and dish up what you want," Kathleen selected a ladle from the drawer for the sauce. "You know the drill. Dinner at my house is informal."

After everyone had served themselves and taken their seats, they joined hands at the kitchen table and Jared said, "Dear Heavenly Father, thank You for all You've given us. Guide us to do what is right and be there for us in our time of need. Amen."

Kathleen murmured, "Amen," thinking about Jared's prayer which was very similar to the one she said each morning before starting her day. Each time she said it she felt stronger, more able to face the problems thrown at her during the course of her day. She had Jared to thank for leading her back to the Lord. Even with Mark's troubles, she felt at peace for the first time since John's death. Her life was falling into place.

"Dad, I was telling Kathleen about the school dance coming up in October. Jeremy asked me to go with him." Hannah took a bite of her spaghetti, her gaze glued to her father.

His eyes round, Jared gulped down a large swallow of iced tea. "A date? At twelve?"

"I'll be thirteen in two months and it isn't really a date. His mom will be driving us to the dance and you can come pick us up."

Jared opened his mouth to say something, but closed it immediately, his eyes still round with disbelief.

"Dad, it's the big fall get-together."

Kathleen, sitting next to Jared, heard him mumble, "That's what I'm afraid of," but she didn't think anyone else heard.

"All the seventh- and eighth-graders are going," Hannah continued.

"All?" Jared tore off a piece of his French bread with more force than was needed.

"Well, everyone who counts. Jeremy is just a good friend. Like you and Kathleen."

Jared's eyes widened even more. His mouth curved down in a frown while his brow was creased with deep lines. He ripped another piece off his bread even though he hadn't eaten the first one. "When is this dance?"

"Two weeks."

"Fine. I'll call Jeremy's mother and arrange the transportation."

Kathleen knew that it had been hard for Jared to accept because she saw the death grip he had on the arm of the chair next to her. She hid her grin by dropping her head and staring down at her plate.

Silence fell over the diners at the table. Kathleen allowed it to continue for five minutes while everyone ate before she asked, "Terry, how's school going for you?"

"Okay. I have Mr. Morrow for a teacher. He's pretty cool. He's the only man teaching at my school."

"I wish there were more men teachers in the elementary schools." Kathleen ate a forkful of spaghetti. "One of Mark's best teachers was a man. Remember your third-grade teacher?"

"Yeah, he was okay."

A clap of thunder rocked the house. Hannah shifted in her chair, staring out the window at the darkness beyond. Branches of a Bradford pear tree scratched the panes as though they were fingernails raking across the glass. Another bright flash of light, then a boom of thunder sounded. The lull in the rain was over, Kathleen thought as she noted the panic-stricken look on the young girl's face.

Wanting to reassure the child, Kathleen touched Hannah's arm. "When Mark had Mr. Horn, he used to come home every day with a new story to tell about something neat they had done at school that day. Did you ever have a man teacher, Hannah?"

Jared's daughter tore her gaze from the window and stared wide-eyed at Kathleen. "Huh?"

Kathleen repeated the question, hoping to take the child's mind off the storm beginning to rage outside.

Hannah shook her head and returned her gaze to the window. Sounds of hail struck the glass with more lightning and thunder vibrating the air. "Daddy, we need to turn on the radio."

Jared glanced at Kathleen who rose and switched on the radio on the kitchen counter. A song finished playing then the announcer came on.

"This just in from the national weather bureau. There has been a tornado sighted near Henderson, Arkansas, heading southeast."

Lightning hit close by. The house shook as the thunder rumbled immediately afterward. The lights flickered several times, then went out. Pitch dark cloaked Kathleen.

Hannah screamed, then began crying. "Dad."

"I'm here, Hannah."

Kathleen heard Jared scrape his chair back. She hurriedly rose and went to the counter where the candles were. She fumbled for the matches and struck one, then lit a large, thick candle. It gave off a soft glow that allowed Kathleen to ignite the others more easily. She took two to the table, leaving the other two spaced out on the counter.

"What about the tornado?" Hannah asked, hugging Jared and burying her face against his forest-green shirt.

"Does the radio have batteries?" he asked, finding Kathleen in the dimness.

She shook her head, wishing she had remembered to buy some at the store a few days ago.

Jared stroked Hannah's back. "We'll be all right. It's only a thunderstorm with hail."

"But the man said something about a tornado," Terry interrupted, his voice high-pitched as the glasses in the cabinet rattled with another round of thunder.

"Daddy," Hannah sobbed.

"Terry, Hannah, we will be fine."

"Come on, everyone. Let's finish our dinner. I've got dessert." Kathleen filled her fork with some spaghetti and put it into her mouth.

No one else did. All eyes watched her while she took a sip of her tea and another bite. Jared started to move back to his chair, but Hannah wouldn't let go.

"What if we skip right to dessert?" Jared asked, settling into Hannah's chair while holding her.

"That's a good idea. I made a double fudge chocolate cake this morning, and I don't want any left. I'll end up eating it and I don't need it."

"No one needs chocolate."

Kathleen exaggerated a shocked expression. "No one needs chocolate! Speak for yourself. Chocolate is what takes people's worries away. Right, Hannah?"

The young girl twisted about so she could look at Kathleen. "Yes," she squeaked out.

"Can you help me with the dessert?"

"I don't —" Hannah swallowed hard. "I guess so." She slid off her father's lap and followed Kathleen to the counter where a cake server sat.

Kathleen reached into the cabinet for the dessert plates. A tornado siren blared, cutting through the sounds of the storm raging outside. In spite of the need to remain calm, Kathleen couldn't keep her heart from racing.

Hannah whirled and dashed back to her father who stood, his face pale in the dim light. She flung herself at him while Terry and Mark came to their feet.

"We have a place under the staircase that probably is the best place to go in case of a tornado." Kathleen started for the door with a flashlight from the drawer lighting the way.

Mark took a candle and grabbed the matches. Jared brought up the rear as they hurried out of the kitchen. Hail spattered the windowpanes. Wind roared. Lightning illuminated the room.

Kathleen opened the door, motioning everyone to go into the small storage room below the staircase. She closed them into the cramped space as another streak of lightning flashed. She scanned the faces staring at her, fear on the children's while Jared's held a fierce determination. His calm composure reinforced hers.

"Sorry about the boxes." Kathleen settled herself on the hardwood floor, leaning against the door. "Mark, push those to the back so you and Terry can sit on the floor. Hannah, there are some blankets in that box. Pull some out and let's make ourselves comfortable."

Trembling, Hannah wrapped herself in a

plaid blanket. "How long do we stay in here?"

Over the sounds of the siren and storm, Jared said, "When the siren goes off, we'll stay in here for a while. Then I'll go out and check to make sure it's safe."

Hannah gripped his arm. "Daddy, you can't go out there. What if the tornado hits while you're out there?" Panic laced each word, her eyes as round as saucers.

He pulled her against his side. "Honey, I won't go until I think it's safe. I promise."

"You know I think there's a deck of cards in that game box back there, Mark. Why don't you get it and we can play a game of Go Fish to pass the time while we wait." Kathleen pointed to a container near her son.

Mark rummaged in the box and produced a deck with a flourish. Kathleen positioned the powerful flashlight so there was enough light to see the cards while Jared shuffled then dealt.

"Daddy, can we say a prayer?" Hannah asked as she scooped up her cards and tried to fan them out. Her hands shook so badly that several fell to the floor.

"That's a great idea. Let's join hands." Jared reached for Hannah's then Kathleen's.

The strong feel of his fingers about hers strengthened Kathleen's ragged nerves. "May I?"

His gaze captured hers and held it. "Please do."

"Lord, we need Your strength now and Your protection. Let no harm come to the town or its people. We offer our thanks in the name of Jesus Christ, our Savior. Amen."

Hannah took several deep breaths, her watery gaze on Kathleen. "Do you think He heard us?"

"He hears all our prayers. We will get through this."

Jared squeezed Kathleen's hand, conveying his support.

One tear slipped down Hannah's cheek. "I don't like storms. Why does it have to rain so hard?"

"Honey, I don't like storms, either." Jared brushed away his daughter's tear.

Hannah shuddered when another loud clap of thunder pierced their haven, reminding them of the storm that raged outside.

"Come on. I've got a great hand, and I bet I'll win this game," Kathleen said. "Terry, why don't you go first?"

As the young boy began to play, Kathleen

offered up another silent prayer that everything would be all right. Not five minutes later the tornado siren stopped. For a long moment no one said anything as though they all waited to see if the siren would start again.

"Do you think it's safe now?" Mark asked, laying his cards down in front of him, the game forgotten.

"I'm sure it is. You all stay here while I go out and check." Jared moved to the door.

"Dad!" Hannah's high-pitched voice cut into the silence. "Don't."

"We can't stay in here." Jared cracked the door open. "I don't hear anything. Even the rain has abated some."

He started out when Hannah added, "Be careful."

Jared closed them in the storage room. Again no one spoke. Hannah chewed on her bottom lip, her gaze riveted to the door. Two minutes later her father reappeared, throwing open the door.

"I think everything is fine. I looked outside in front and no houses had any damage except some tree branches down in the yards."

As they exited the small room under the staircase, the lights flickered on then off then on again. The warm glow emanating from the kitchen drew Kathleen toward it. In spite of the storm, she was amazed at how well the evening had gone. They had felt like a blended family, having an adventure, making the best of a difficult situation. Dare she dream of more?

Kathleen stood next to Jared in the church parking lot and surveyed the storm damage. There was a nip in the air from a cool front that had pushed through with the rain. The night before their church hadn't fared as well as she and her neighbors. The yard and gardens surrounding it were littered with tree branches and leaves. Some plants were uprooted and debris cluttered the area. One small oak had split and fallen on a swing set. A white pine had crashed into a window in one of the classrooms and rainwater covered the floor.

"There's a lot of work to be done," Kathleen murmured as other parishioners arrived to help clean up the mess.

"It could have been worse." Jared reached into his car and began to unload some of his tools he'd brought.

Kathleen took a rake and a shovel from him. "Some of the towns around here weren't as lucky as Crystal Springs."

"Thankfully the damage is to property

and no one was hurt from the two torna-does."

"How's Hannah doing today?" Kathleen noticed the young girl with some other children taking trash bags to pick up the litter.

"Since the sky is cloudless, much better. She's been scared of thunderstorms all her life. When she was five, we had a bad storm with several tornadoes that came through this area. A couple of people were hurt. One was our neighbor. She never got over it."

"To tell you the truth if it hadn't been for the children you would have seen my panic, too."

"Believe it or not, Hannah was better last night than she usually is. As I've said before, you're a good influence on her." Jared watched Mark take a garbage bag and begin to tidy up his area of the churchyard. "How's Mark's therapy?"

"The doctor is pleased with his progress. We caught his illness early, which is good. Mark even told me this morning that he'll play for the children at the hospital. He's starting to practice on his guitar again."

Jared began walking toward the children's playground. "The volunteer program is really picking up. In the morning you have the ladies of the church volunteering and in the afternoon the teenagers. Not bad for only doing it six weeks."

"It seems everyone wanted to volunteer, but no one wanted to volunteer to coordinate it. I like organizing things." A flush of pride took hold of Kathleen. She enjoyed her volunteer job because she was good at it and she still had time to be there for Mark when he needed her.

"You have quite a knack for it."

"Well, thank you, kind sir. It's nice to use my talent for a worthy cause."

For the next few hours Kathleen worked alongside Jared cleaning up the playground before moving to the garden where Mark and Terry were. The young boy held the leaf bag open as Mark scooped up the debris and put it inside. Kathleen was glad to see that Terry wasn't afraid of Mark anymore.

"Do you really mean it? You'll show me how to play the guitar?" Terry asked Mark, following him to another pile of leaves and branches.

"Sure. Why not? Next time you're over I'll give you your first lesson."

Terry caught sight of his father. "Can we visit Mark and Kathleen today after we finish here?"

"Son, you shouldn't invite yourself over to other people's houses."

Terry's face fell. "But, Dad, Mark says

he'll teach me to play the guitar."

"Terry, you can come over anytime it's okay with your father." Kathleen leaned close to Jared and lowered her voice, "I have a pot of chili on and you and your family are welcome to share it with us this evening."

With his blue eyes gleaming, Jared angled his head so he could look straight into her face. "Mrs. Davis has been complaining we aren't home enough to eat her cooking. But I won't turn down a pot of homemade chili even for the sake of keeping my housekeeper happy."

"Good. Then it's settled. After we finish here, give me an hour to clean up and then come on over."

Jared's gaze skimmed down her length, the gleam brightening. "You look fine just the way you are."

She was aware of Mark and Terry listening now to their conversation. The heat of a blush flamed her cheeks. She twisted about so her back was to the boys. "It may be cooler since the storm yesterday, but I promise you I have worked up a sweat."

Jared started to reply when Terry cut in. "Dad, does this mean we're going to eat at their house tonight?"

Without taking his gaze off her, Jared said, "Yes."

A loud yippee punctuated the air followed by Terry racing toward the parking lot, yelling back, "I'm gonna tell Hannah."

"I think you've made my family happy." He bent toward her until only inches separated them. "And you've made me happy."

Her stomach did a flip-flop. His nearness produced a quickening pace of her heartbeat. She realized in that moment that next to her son, Jared and his children were the most important people in her life. She wanted to be the cause of their joy. Jared had struggled for years, giving of himself to others and his children. He deserved some happiness in his life. Maybe she was the one to bring him that.

In the past few months she had discovered what she wanted most in life was to be a wife and mother. For a time she had lost her identity after John's death, but that was only because she was trying to be someone different — to put some distance between her old life and her new one. Denying what made her happy, though, caused her situation to be worse. She wasn't going to do that anymore.

She and Jared had settled into a comfortable relationship since the beginning of school. She didn't have to rely on him as she had done in the summer when she was at such a loss with Mark and his illness. Jared had given her the means to tackle her problems on her own and for that she would always be grateful. Now she wanted to help him as he had her — if he would allow her into his heart completely.

After placing a folder on her desk at the hospital, Kathleen turned to leave her office. The bright sunshine streaming through her window drew her. She looked out at the garden below, some of the trees bare, some with their leaves colored orange, red and yellow.

November would be here in a couple of days. In a few weeks she'd have been back in Crystal Springs for six months. So much had happened in such a short amount of time. She'd met Jared and her life had taken a turn for the better. Her son was recovering, getting some of his life back. There were days when he seemed almost as normal as before. She owed her new outlook on life to her renewed faith in the Lord and to Jared.

A male cardinal with his mate landed on a bare branch of a maple tree. His vivid red stood out against the brown landscape like a ray of hope. As she watched the pair fly off, she knew she would be all right, that the

Lord was with her even through the rough times. She had abandoned him, but He hadn't abandoned her. With Jared's help, though, she'd rediscovered the power of His love.

A rap at her door, then Jared opening it and sticking his head into her office pulled her away from her musings. "I'm coming. I wouldn't miss this for the world." Kathleen hurried toward Jared.

"The kids have everything set up. The patients are in place."

"Great. I hope everything goes all right with Mark's performance."

Jared grasped her hand, linking his fingers through hers. "It will. His medicine seems to be working. He's doing well in his therapy. This will be good for him."

Kathleen started down the hall toward the rec room on the pediatrics floor. "I hope so. It was his idea."

In the room, children in wheelchairs, on crutches and even one in a portable bed waited for the first act to begin. The teenagers from the youth group had worked up a show for them. Mark was the third performer. Kathleen barely registered the first two teenagers at the front of the crowded rec room.

Then Mark came out and stood before

the twenty people in the audience. He smiled tentatively and sat on a stool, positioning his guitar in his lap. Staring at his hands, he began to play "Eleanor Rigby" by the Beatles. Rigid in her chair, Kathleen held her breath through the first verse. By the second verse she forced herself to take deep breaths, clasping her hands tightly together. Toward the end of the song Mark missed a chord. He stopped. Fear pounded in her chest. She started to rise to go to him when he began to play again, picking up where he left off. She released a long sigh. When Mark finished the last note, she collapsed back against the chair, prying her fingers apart to clap.

"He did great," Jared whispered as Mark took his bows midst the loud applause. One patient blew a piercing whistle. Mark reddened, then left the impromptu stage.

"Yes, he did," she murmured, the tension siphoning out of her. She felt like a wet noodle.

While the rest of the teenagers continued to perform, she slipped out of the room to find Mark. He stood at the window at the end of the hallway, staring down at the street.

"Mark?"

Her son didn't turn or say anything.

She stepped closer and asked, "Mark, are you all right?"

He flinched and whirled about. "I didn't hear you." His face screwed into a frown.

"What's wrong?" Worry surged to the foreground.

Her son shook his head, his frown dissipating. "Nothing. I'm just tired. I've been practicing a lot lately. I didn't want to mess up."

"You were great. The patients loved you."

He lifted his shoulders in a shrug. "Yeah, I guess."

"Honey, there's no guessing about it. Did you hear their applause?"

"Applause? Yes, their applause." Mark clutched his old guitar to his chest. "Let's go home. I'm hungry."

"We could get something at the diner across the street. I bet they still have some of their doughnuts you like so much."

"No, I want to go home." Mark started down the hall toward the elevator.

Kathleen watched him shuffle, her concern increasing. Jared came out into the corridor and said something to Mark as he passed him. Her son stopped at the elevator and turned to wait for her.

She paused by Jared and said in a lowered

voice, "He says he's tired so I'm taking him home."

"If you need me, all you have to do is call."

"I know. Thanks." Kathleen offered him a smile before heading toward her son who leaned against the wall, his gaze boring a hole into the floor by his feet.

Maybe Mark had done too much too fast. She had to remember it wasn't quite four months ago that her son was diagnosed with schizophrenia and stress and tension could aggravate it.

At the elevator she glanced back at Jared, his warm gaze intent on her. He had been there for her and her son from the beginning. His unselfishness and compassion had touched the cold core about her heart and melted it. As she stepped onto the elevator and waited for the doors to swish closed, she realized she loved Dr. Jared Matthews, that she wanted to be his wife and mother to his children.

CHAPTER TWELVE

"I'll have my cell phone with me, Mark. If you need me for anything, call. I've written the number down by the phone as well as Aunt Laura's and Grandma's."

"I know their numbers. I'm not a baby. I'm fine, Mom." With a dour expression, Mark opened the refrigerator and inspected its contents. Finally he chose an apple to eat and closed the door. Taking a bite, he added, "Really."

"I know. The doctor has been pleased." After he had played at the hospital the week before, she had made sure he had gone to his therapy session with Dr. Martins to make sure everything was all right.

"See. What have I been telling you. It's not like you haven't left me alone before. I'm sixteen. I can stay by myself."

"Okay. I'll stop worrying," Kathleen said, even though she knew in her heart that would be impossible.

Mark grinned. "That'll be the day." He bit into the apple again.

Kathleen stepped out into the middle of the kitchen and did a turn, the soft silk dress billowing about her knees. "How do I look?"

"Beautiful, Mom. Green is your best color."

Mark tossed the half-eaten apple into the trash can, then began rummaging through the pantry. Kathleen noticed his favorite shirt needed a button and several new stains donned the front. She started to say something when the doorbell rang.

Mark grabbed some cookies and said, "I'm out of here."

Kathleen answered the door as her son pounded up the stairs as though he were a member of an elephant herd. She greeted Jared with a smile.

"Everything okay?" One of his brows rose at the sound of Mark's door slamming closed.

"Just Mark being his usual graceful self. He's growing so fast sometimes I wonder if he knows what to do with his arms and legs. He —" Kathleen's voice trailed off into silence as Jared produced a beautiful bouquet of yellow roses from behind his back.

"For me?" she asked, more in wonderment than in query.

"Are there any other ladies living here?"

She shook her head, her throat contracting at the gesture. "How did you know yellow roses were my favorite flowers?" She took them from his outstretched hand, cradling them to her while smelling their sweet fragrance.

"A certain young man who is all arms and legs told me."

She remembered the special occasions John would bring her yellow roses. After he had died, she hadn't thought she would ever receive them again from a man — a man she had come to love dearly.

"May I come in?"

She laughed, realizing she blocked the entrance. Stepping to the side, she took another deep breath, the roses perfuming the air.

Jared strode into the living room without another word.

Puzzled, Kathleen followed. "Don't we have to be at the hospital soon?"

"Yes, but I wanted to talk to you in private before we go. Why don't you put the flowers in some water first?"

"Fine. I'll be right back." Kathleen hurried into the kitchen and found a crystal vase.

After filling it with water, she unwrapped the cellophane from around the bouquet and began to arrange the flowers in the vase. Something caught the light and glittered. She searched the roses and discovered a diamond ring, square-shaped, tied to a thornless stem. With quivering fingers, she loosened the yellow ribbon and nestled the beautiful one-carat diamond ring in her palm. She shook so much she had to steady her hand with her other one.

"Will you marry me, Kathleen Somers?"

His deep, rich voice penetrated the quiet of the kitchen. With tears welling in her eyes, she spun about. One tear rolled down her cheek as she offered him a smile. Her throat was so tight all she could do was nod.

Jared covered the space between them in three quick strides and drew her into his arms. "I love you and I want you to be in my life, in my children's lives."

Tears of joy continued to flow as she stared at the beautiful ring cradled in her hand. "I wasn't expecting this."

"From the beginning I knew you were special. Getting to know you these past months has only reconfirmed that feeling. Hannah and Terry think the world of you. Their father does, too."

She lifted her gaze to his and saw in his expression the love he talked about. "I never thought it was possible to be so lucky twice in my life. After my husband died, I had resigned myself to living alone. You have changed all that."

Jared took the ring and slipped it on her left hand, then framed her face. When his lips settled over hers, all her love went into the kiss. It was as though a choir of angels surrounded them, their voices raised in glorious song.

When he pulled back, he combed his fingers through her short hair. "We have a lot to talk about, but right now we have a banquet to go to. If I wasn't being honored as the doctor of the year, I'd rather stay right here kissing you."

That thought sent a delicious streak down her length. "But since you are, we'd better get going. We wouldn't want anyone to worry that you weren't going to show up."

Jared chuckled, hooking his arm about her shoulder. "I did threaten Dr. Curtis that I wouldn't."

"You should feel honored the hospital is naming you doctor of the year."

"I am. But I told Dr. Curtis all they had to do was give me a plaque for my office."

"To go with the other two you've received."

"Mrs. Somers, I do think you are trying to get me to blush."

Kathleen glanced up at his flushed cheeks. "I think it's working."

"Yes, well, I'm going to tell everyone it's because of the crisp, fall air." He opened her front door.

Outside Kathleen took a deep breath of that crisp, fall air. Someone had a fire going to grill steaks. Her mouth watered. "I'm hungry. I hope they have all the speeches after we eat."

"Of course, and mine will be blessedly short."

"The masses have come to hear you speak on the future of medicine. You can't disappoint us." Kathleen slid into the front seat of Jared's car.

Jared laughed. "The masses are coming for a free dinner."

When Jared settled behind the steering wheel, Kathleen said, "You have underestimated your appeal, Dr. Matthews."

He clasped her hand. "Tonight is special because you have agreed to be my wife."

For a few seconds Kathleen allowed her doubts to invade her mind. Did he love her or the idea of her as his children's mother? Was it fair to saddle him with Mark and his chronic illness? Then she looked at his handsome profile and shook the doubts from her thoughts, determined not to let anything spoil her evening.

Jared finished his short speech with a humble thank you. Rising, Kathleen joined in the loud applause that filled the banquet room. From the dais she scanned the audience and saw the same genuine appreciation for Jared's accomplishments that she felt. After taking the plaque, Jared shook Dr. Curtis's hand then made his way back to his seat next to her.

"Let's get out of here," he whispered.

"I do believe you're blushing again, Dr. Matthews."

"It's the heat in this room. They must have the furnace cranked up real high."

"I'm quite comfortable."

"I bet you are. You didn't have to get up in front of seventy-five people and make a speech."

"Anyone who can handle twenty-five rowdy teenagers can handle a small crowd of seventy-five." Kathleen gathered her shawl and beaded purse.

"Speak for yourself." He touched the small of her back to guide her off the dais.

They began to make their way to the back of the room, but at every table Jared had to stop to acknowledge congratulations. Everyone wanted to talk to him, adding their pleasure at his engagement when they saw the ring on Kathleen's finger. She found herself blushing at the compliments they received, as bad as Jared about being the center of attention.

When they finally escaped the banquet room, Jared retrieved their overcoats from his office and helped Kathleen into hers. "I promised Terry and Hannah I would bring you by tonight. We don't have to stay long, but they wanted to see the ring on your finger."

"So did everyone know about you proposing tonight but me?"

"Mrs. Miller saw me at the jewelry store buying the ring today. I knew I had to act fast when I couldn't evade her questions about what I was doing. I had planned to take you out sailing and propose then."

Kathleen halted her progress to his car, facing him. "I wouldn't trade the way you proposed for anything."

"Still I'm surprised you didn't hear before I arrived. Your sister called me up and questioned me before I left to pick you up."

"Laura knows?"

"As well as your parents."

"I guess I'll have to call them when I get home."

"They're waiting for a call, no matter how

late you come home. They made me promise you would call them."

In his car she said, "I love being the last person to find out something."

"Blame Mrs. Miller. She's the worst gossiper I know."

"And a good friend of my mother's. I'm sure she hurried home and called up Mom."

"I think that's how Laura told me she found out — from your mother." Jared pulled out of the parking lot. "Crystal Springs isn't a small town, but it's not a large city, either. I sometimes forget how close-knit the community is."

Ten minutes later Jared stopped in his driveway and rounded the front of his car to open the passenger door for Kathleen. He took her hand and held it while walking up the steps to his door. Before he had a chance to put his key in the lock, Hannah threw the door open.

"You said yes?" the young girl asked, an eager expression on her face.

Smiling, Kathleen nodded.

Leaping into the air, Terry cheered behind Hannah.

Hannah flung herself at Kathleen, her arms winding around her in a hug that threatened to overwhelm Kathleen in its enthusiasm. "I'm so glad. I just knew you would. Dad is the best."

"I agree." Kathleen peered at Jared, the gleam in his eyes seizing her in its depth. Just from a mere look she felt her insides go all mushy.

Hannah tugged Kathleen into the house. "I want to see the ring on your finger." She grabbed Kathleen's hand and lifted it toward the light so that her brother could see, too. "It's beautiful. I got to help Dad."

The thought of Hannah shopping for a wedding ring with Jared dissolved any reservations she might have had. She'd always wanted a larger family and now she would have it. She couldn't ask for nicer children than Hannah and Terry. Everything would work itself out.

"I must say both you and your father have great taste."

Terry clasped her other hand. "We made a cake to celebrate. Come on." He began pulling her toward the kitchen.

Kathleen glanced back at Jared who shrugged and said, "I didn't know anything about this."

"It's a surprise for both of you." Hannah took her father's hand. "Mrs. Davis didn't even help us. I promised her I would clean up before she went to her room to watch TV."

When Kathleen entered the kitchen, she stopped dead in her tracks, stunned. The room was spotless and the only evidence that anything had been made was the chocolate cake sitting in the middle of the table. Her eyes filled with tears at the sweet gesture from Jared's two children.

"I don't know what to say." Kathleen swallowed several times. "Thank you, Hannah and Terry. This is the nicest thing you could have done for me."

She slanted a look toward Jared who was as surprised as she was. He didn't say anything. She could tell by his watery eyes and deep inhalations that he was having a hard time controlling his emotions as well.

"Come on. Cut the cake. I want some." Terry dragged Kathleen toward the table where a knife and four small plates sat next to the cake.

"So do I." Even though Kathleen tried not to have too many sweets, there was no way she wouldn't eat some of this cake.

After slicing four pieces and putting them on the plates, she handed one to Terry then Hannah. She saved the last one for Jared who moved slowly to the table and sat next to her.

Composed now, he cut his first bite and brought it to his mouth. "Mmm. Delicious.

This is the best cake I've ever tasted."

"Oh, Dad, you're just saying that." Hannah delved into her piece and had half the cake gone in two minutes.

Terry didn't bother to say a word. He was too busy eating. When he was finished, he looked up and asked, "Can I have another piece?" His chin was smeared with chocolate icing.

Kathleen gave him a napkin while she sliced him another small section. "I have to agree with your dad. This is great. I'd like to take some home for Mark. Is that okay?" she asked Hannah.

The young girl nodded, her mouth full of cake. She went to a drawer and removed some foil, then cut a big slice for Mark and wrapped it up.

For a minute everyone sat at the table, staring at the half-eaten cake, not saying a word. The feeling of family permeated the room, Kathleen's heart swelling with the knowledge that soon they would all be a family.

She sighed. "Speaking of Mark, I'd better get home. I told him I would be back by ten."

"And you two need to clean this up, then get to bed." Jared rose.

"Do we have to? This is a special occasion." Hannah's mouth curved down in a pout.

"Yes. This may be Saturday, but we have church tomorrow."

Hannah grumbled but stood. Terry ran his finger down the knife to get off some of the chocolate cake stuck on the blade, then popped the sweet lump into his mouth, making a loud smacking noise.

"I'll be back soon. I expect you two to be tucked snug in your beds."

Hannah turned the water on as Kathleen and Jared left the kitchen, Kathleen holding the piece of cake for Mark as though it was a treasure.

"I'm so touched by what those two did," Kathleen said as she stepped out onto the porch. Not even the cold air could chase away the warm glow that cocooned her.

"So am I. I never imagined something like that." Jared closed the front door, paused, shaking his head. "They continually amaze me."

"I think that's a given with children. They're always doing the unexpected. Mark will enjoy the cake. He loves chocolate."

Her house was only five minutes away. When Jared pulled into the driveway, she noticed the lights were off in Mark's bedroom. "Do you want to come in? I think we should tell Mark together."

"He already knows."

"He does? I guess I was the last person to know your plans. What if I had said no?"

"I would have kept asking until I got the right answer."

Even in the darkness of the car, Kathleen knew that Jared had flashed her an impish grin, his two dimples appearing. "Well, Mark doesn't know what my answer was."

"True. I can't stay long, but I agree we should tell him together."

She loved hearing him say the word *together*. It made the feeling she'd experienced in his kitchen deepen even more and confirmed in her mind that she was doing the right thing by accepting his proposal.

They walked side by side up to her front door. She unlocked it and went in first. Inside the sound of Mark's CD player drifted down to her. He must be in his bedroom even though his lights were off. She was glad he was listening to his music again.

"I'll go get him." Kathleen hurried up the stairs, mindful that Jared's gaze was on her the whole way up. That awareness sent a tingling sensation down her spine.

At her son's door, she knocked. No answer. She rapped on the wood again. Still nothing. Heart rate increasing, she pushed open the door and entered. At first she thought the room was empty, then she saw her son and her stomach plummeted.

Mark huddled in the corner with his hands clasping his ears. Curled into a tight ball, he didn't move when she switched off the CD player. Her legs shook as she crossed the room to kneel next to her son. When she placed her hand on his shoulder, he shrank away, whimpering.

Alarm shot through her. "Mark?"

"Make it stop. Make the voices go away."

"I turned off the music."

He shook his head violently. "No, I still hear the voices."

From deep inside a calmness descended over Kathleen. She could deal with this. God was with her. "Mark, you need to come with me."

"No, I can't!"

Kathleen held out her hand. "I can make the voices go away. Just come with me." She pitched her voice to a soothing level.

Mark bolted to his feet, his arms stiff at his sides, his hands balled. "I can't! They're waiting to get me."

The hysterical ring to his declaration confirmed to Kathleen what she must do. "Okay, then why don't you lie down. Relax."

With eyes round he looked at his bed. "Can't. Snakes are on it. Don't want to die."

She hated to leave Mark even for a moment, but she needed Jared's help. She headed for the door.

"Where are you going?" Mark's voice was a shrill.

"I'm going to get someone to help me catch the snakes." She knew it was useless to argue with Mark that there were no snakes on his bed. In his mind he believed it and that was all that mattered.

"Hurry." Her son slid down the wall and curled himself into a tight ball, his hands clasped over his ears again, his face hidden.

Kathleen rushed to the top of the stairs. "Jared. Jared, I need you."

He appeared at the bottom of the steps. "What's wrong?"

"Mark's having an episode. He's hearing voices and seeing snakes. He won't leave his room."

"I'll get my bag from the car and be right up." Jared hurried out the front door.

Kathleen quickly made her way to her son's room, relieved to find him still in the corner where she had left him. She called his name, but he didn't respond. She decided to wait until Jared was there to do anything else. Moving closer, she watched Mark for any change.

Jared entered not two minutes later with the black bag he always had with him in case of an emergency. Mark didn't move even when Jared said his name.

"I'm going to sedate him, then we need to get him to the hospital and figure out what's going on," Jared whispered so Mark couldn't hear.

"He was doing so well."

Jared prepared the injection while Kathleen monitored her son. When Jared was ready to give him the shot, Kathleen approached Mark.

"Honey, did we get all the snakes?" Kathleen asked, hoping to focus his attention on her.

Mark peered at his bed, his face screwed into a scowl. "No. They keep coming from under the bed."

Jared managed to inject Mark in the arm while Kathleen hovered nearby in case her son resisted. Mark stared down at the needle being pulled from him. His wide-eyed gaze flashed back to Kathleen.

Shock registered on his face for only a few seconds, then he exploded, leaping to his feet and scrambling away from them and his bed. "Stay away from me. You're part of them."

"Honey, all that was for was to help the voices and the snakes go away. Relax." Again she made sure her voice was level, calm.

"No, you poisoned me!" He began to dart for the door, stopped halfway there and spun about. "I can't leave! Snakes are everywhere." Frightened, he backed up into another corner and stood on tiptoes as though he was trying to get away from something crawling on the floor. "Make them go away!"

"How much longer, Jared?"

"Not long."

Her son collapsed to the floor and hunched over, covering his head as though protecting himself. Slowly the rigid set to his body eased and he lay down on the carpeted floor.

"Let's try to get him to leave now." Cautiously Jared approached Mark.

Kathleen took her son on one side while Jared held him propped up on the other. They helped Mark to his feet, his expression dazed, his eyes unfocused.

Kathleen started to say something reassuring to her son, then decided that might set him off. Instead, she and Jared walked him from his bedroom and down the stairs, each step labored, with them supporting more and more of her son's weight.

In the entry hall she snatched up her purse, wondering when she and Mark would be home again. One of the happiest days of her life was ending tragically.

The quiet comfort of the hospital chapel drew Kathleen. She pushed open the door and stepped into the sanctuary. Sitting in the front pew, she bowed her head and said, "Lord, thank You for being there for my son and myself. Thank You for Jared's presence when I needed him most last night. With Your support I will make it through this latest crisis. Mark will get better."

Kathleen settled back on the pew to take a few minutes to let the silence sink in. She was tired after a busy night dealing with Mark's latest episode, but relieved to discover that it had been brought on because her son had stopped taking his medication. She would have to monitor that more closely, but she could do it. She could do whatever was necessary to help her son get better. She knew that now. Knowing the Lord was with her every step of the way made this emergency easier for her. Thinking back to the last time Mark had been in the hospital four months ago, she realized she was much stronger now due to her renewed faith.

Rising, she left the chapel, as refreshed as though she had rested for a few hours rather than a few minutes. She wanted to be there when Mark woke up this morning. Her son would stay in the hospital a couple of days to get his medication straightened out and for observation, then they would go home and begin again.

Out in the hall she saw Jared striding toward her. The scowl on his face set off an alarm in her. She waited by the double doors into the chapel.

"I thought I might find you here," Jared said, taking her elbow and guiding her toward a waiting room across from the chapel.

No one was in the area. Bright sunshine flooded the room with warmth even though it was cold outside. The sterile furnishings didn't offer any amenities. Kathleen remained standing, puzzled by the expression on Jared's face.

"Is something else wrong with Mark?" she asked when Jared released his hold on her and began to pace the small room.

He stopped, spun about and plunged his hand through his hair.

"Wrong? Not now. Dr. Martins says he should be okay if he stays on his medication.

I should have seen this coming. I could have prevented this."

"Is that why you're upset?" The calmness that had assisted her the evening before was firmly in place now.

"Don't you think I have a good reason for being upset? I'm a doctor. I know people start to feel better and decide to stop taking their medication. They don't think they need it anymore. I should have warned you, watched for the signs. Mark shouldn't have had this relapse."

Stunned by the vehement tone in his voice, Kathleen stared at Jared, her teeth digging into her bottom lip. While tending to Mark and making sure he got the care he needed, Jared had been composed, calm, professional. Now, however, he was as upset as though he personally blamed himself for everything that happened to Mark the past eighteen hours. She thought about how Jared's wife's death had taken a grave toll on him. She suspected he still blamed himself for what she had done to herself even though he hadn't said anything about it in several months. In her happiness about his proposal she had pushed that to the back of her mind.

"You aren't Mark's keeper. You weren't at fault. I'm through trying to blame someone for my problems. It does no good and can certainly do a lot of harm."

His eyes clouded with an expression of agony. "I promised you I would help you. I should have seen it coming."

Kathleen closed the distance between them and took his hands within hers. "Why are you so hard on yourself?"

"I'm a doctor," he said, agitated, as though that would clarify everything.

"And you are only human. We can't see into the future. We can only do what we feel is our best at the moment."

"But I didn't." He pulled his hands from hers, his fingers delving into his hair as he backed away. "I've let you down and I've let Mark down." He pivoted and left the waiting room.

Kathleen watched Jared stride down the corridor toward the elevators. Chewing on her bottom lip, she wished she could wipe away his pain. She wasn't sure she could. She wasn't sure if anyone could — only Jared. And she didn't think he was ready to do that. He was still wrestling with his guilt over his wife's death. He still blamed himself for her drinking problem. *How can I ask him to take on a problem like Mark's?*

Her son's illness was long-term and serious. She didn't know when or if he would go into remission. She didn't know when or if he would have another relapse. She did realize she would never knowingly add to Jared's pain. He had taken care of his wife for years, dealing with her alcoholism, trying to make their marriage work, trying to give his children a good home, and the whole time feeling as though he had let his family down because he couldn't fix his wife's problem.

Instead of going back to Mark's room, Kathleen walked to the chapel doors and went inside. She needed to do some soul-searching. She loved Jared with all her heart, but she wasn't sure that getting married to her was best for Jared.

When her doorbell rang that evening, Kathleen drew in a deep, calming breath and headed to the entry hall to answer it. She knew it was Jared because she had asked him to come over. With a trembling hand, she reached out and touched the knob. Again she inhaled deeply, trying to ignore the throbbing ache in her heart.

When she swung the door open, she forced a smile of greeting to her lips. "That was fast."

"I was on my way home when I received your call."

The haggard lines about his face ripped through the composure she was trying to maintain. Jared had been at the hospital most of the night before and probably hadn't slept more than a few hours, if that. When he looked at her, she saw exhaustion in his face, but beneath that she glimpsed his anguish. He had become a doctor to save the world and when he couldn't, he blamed himself.

"Your call sounded urgent. Did something else happen to Mark?"

"No, when I left him at the hospital, he was awake and doing okay. We need to talk."

He frowned, but didn't say anything.

"Let's sit in the living room." Kathleen desperately needed to sit before her legs gave out. Without waiting to see if Jared followed, she walked into the room and settled herself in a chair across from the couch. Distance was important to maintain for what she had to say to Jared.

He slowly entered, stared at the large, empty sofa, then at her. He sat, clasping his hands together, his elbows resting on his thighs. "What do we need to talk about?" The question came out stiffly, each word laced with tension.

Her heart beat frantically against her

chest. Her composure was quickly slipping away. She crossed her legs then uncrossed them, the whisper of denim sounding loud in the sudden silence.

Finally she realized the only way she could do this was to just do it. "Jared, I want to call off our engagement."

CHAPTER THIRTEEN

Jared blinked. "Why?" The question held an underlying tension that slowly fell over his features, too.

"I don't think this will work between us. I —" She glanced away from the intensity in his expression and searched for a way to explain her decision. *Please, God, help me to make him understand.*

"What has changed since yesterday, Kathleen?" He straightened, nothing casual about his posture.

She rose, needing to move, to put some space between them, before she gave in to her desire to be his wife. "I won't be responsible for you feeling trapped in our marriage."

"Trapped?" He, too, stood but remained by the couch.

"Yes. Mark's relapse has made me realize that my son may always need more help than most children. I don't want you to feel trapped because of Mark. I've seen what your marriage to Alice did to you. I couldn't stand for that to happen to our marriage."

"That was a different situation. How can you compare the two?"

"Is it so different? From the beginning you have used Mark's illness as a personal crusade. You've been determined to find out what was wrong with him and fix it. Don't tell me you don't blame yourself for Mark's relapse."

"I don't —" Jared snapped his mouth closed, the line of his jaw forbidding.

"That's a burden I won't be responsible for. I couldn't stand by and see that happen. It would —" She halted, unable to tell him how much it would destroy her. She loved him too much to be a part of that. Tears blurred her vision. She turned away, trying to compose herself long enough to explain. She'd had a wonderful marriage with John. She knew what was possible, but not if her son came between them.

She felt the drill of Jared's gaze and slowly faced him, dragging in lungfuls of air. "Marriage is forever. I have to think of Mark. My son may have other relapses. He may not. I don't know." Her throat closed around the last words. Before she lost her nerve, she twisted the engagement ring off her finger and held it out to Jared.

He stared at it for a long moment, his

hands stiffening then flexing into a ball. Finally he snatched the ring and curled his fingers around it. "It doesn't have to be like this."

"I saw how you reacted today. You can't control everything. People will get ill. Luckily most will get well, but not everyone. You think you're responsible for everyone in your life."

"That's my job — to make people better."

"And what happens if you can't? That's what eats you up inside. You're not God. You don't control life and death. I won't have you feeling responsible for Mark's illness. I can't do that to you. Mark needs me right now."

His eyes narrowed, the rigid set of his shoulders attesting to his anger. "And you don't think I do?"

She wanted to go to him and throw herself into his arms. She didn't. It wouldn't solve the problem. Mark would still be ill, and Jared would still feel he had to solve all of her son's problems or else. She was afraid of the "or else." She knew in his heart he still hadn't forgiven himself for his wife's illness or her death.

Jared slid the ring into his coat pocket, then strode toward the front door without another word. As he left, the door clicking shut reverberated through Kathleen's mind. So final.

She hugged her arms to her, a coldness burrowing into the marrow of her bones. Suddenly she wasn't sure how she was going to make it without Jared's support. The urge to go after him prodded her forward. She placed her hand on the door knob and started to turn it.

No! It wouldn't be fair to Jared. I need to learn to stand on my own two feet. I have my family. I have the Lord. I can do this. I have been doing it.

Her hand slipped from the knob, and she pivoted away from the door. She would do what she had first come to Crystal Springs to accomplish: she would create a life for herself and Mark here. Her son's illness didn't change that.

But as she climbed the stairs and walked down the hall, she felt empty inside. Entering her bedroom, she crossed to the night stand and retrieved her Bible. Inside its pages was the solace she needed. With trembling hands, she opened to the story of Ruth.

Jared prowled his den, exhausted but too keyed up to sit and relax. Everyone was in bed, had been when he had finally arrived home. He should have gone to sleep hours ago, but all he could think about was his last meeting with Kathleen earlier that evening. Anger churned his stomach and stretched his patience. Frustrated, he pounded his fists into the back cushion of the wing chair.

"Dad, what's wrong?" Hannah asked.

He whirled at the sound of his daughter's voice. "You should be in bed," he said in a rougher voice than he intended.

Standing in the doorway in her pajamas, her hair messy, her brow wrinkled, his daughter blinked several times. "I wanted to know how Mark was. Kathleen said he would be coming home soon, but still —" Hannah stopped talking, her frown deepening. "Is something wrong with Mark?"

"He'll be okay. He should leave the hospital day after tomorrow."

"Then why were you punching the chair?" Hannah shuffled into the room, wearing her big furry bunny slippers.

Jared stared at them for a moment, reminded that his daughter was still a young girl but at the same time growing into a young woman. And as she grew up and became more independent, he would lose control and influence in her life. That realization left an unsettling feeling in the pit of his stomach.

"Dad?"

"Hannah, come over here and sit next to me. I have something I want to talk to you about." Jared sat on the couch and waited until his daughter plopped down beside him before continuing, "I know you've been looking forward to Kathleen and Mark joining our family, but Kathleen and I aren't engaged anymore."

Surprise widened her eyes. "Why not? You love her. She loves you. I know it. She told me."

"She did?"

Hannah nodded.

Pain pierced through his heart. "Sometimes it takes more than love to make a marriage work."

"Why?"

That's a good question. He put his arm around his daughter and drew her to him. Her presence comforted him and gave him the strength to try and explain. "Two people have to be able to live together. In fact, when two families merge, all the people have to be able to live together."

"We can do that. I know Mark is having problems, but Terry and I have discussed it. We can help him get better. That's what families do." She twisted so she could look up into Jared's face. "When Mom died, you helped me and Terry. You're good at that."

He was? He didn't feel he was at the moment. He felt his life was unraveling, seam by seam. When his younger brother had drowned, he hadn't been able to save him. He hadn't been able to help Alice and now Kathleen was turning him away. Why couldn't he control his life better than this? Why couldn't he save the people who meant so much to him?

Hannah yawned. "Dad, I love you. You're the best."

He gave her a hug, his throat tight with feelings he wished he could contain and place into a nice little box to be pulled out at his command. He had become quite good at that with Alice, but Kathleen had changed all that. His emotions lay bare before the world — before her. "I think a certain young lady is sleepy and needs to go back to bed." Kissing the top of her head, he rose and helped his daughter to her feet. "We'll talk some more tomorrow."

At the door to the den Hannah glanced back. "Talk with Kathleen. We can live as one family."

He wanted to tell his daughter it wasn't him that had backed out of the engagement, that he wasn't the one who had the problem. But the words clogged in his throat and in his heart he wondered if they were true. He eased down onto the couch, rested his head on the back cushion and stared at the white ceiling.

Was Kathleen right? God had given him a powerful talent to help people who were hurting and sick, but He had the ultimate control over who lived and died. Not him. Could he truly accept that and make peace with his past?

When the door to Mark's hospital room opened, Kathleen looked toward the person entering. Jared. Her breath caught in her throat and her pulse quickened. She'd hoped not to see him for a while. She needed time to get her emotions under control, to lock her love for him away in the dark recesses of her heart.

Jared stopped on the other side of her son's bed. "How are you doing today, Mark?"

"Okay. I don't know what —" Mark's voice faded and he stared down at the white sheet, plucking at it. "Thanks for helping me."

"Anytime. I heard you would be leaving here tomorrow."

Mark nodded, his head still bent forward.

"I need to borrow your mom for the afternoon. Is that okay with you? I brought your aunt Laura to keep you company."

Mark lifted his gaze to Jared's. A silent message passed between them that Kathleen wasn't quite sure of. Male bonding?

"Sure."

When Jared rounded the end of the bed, Kathleen frowned. "I do believe I have a say in this. I don't like being the last person in on a secret."

Jared moved into her personal space and took her hand. "You need to work on your control issues. I've certainly had to lately."

His gaze pinned her down, his words held her immobile.

"Mom, you should go with Jared. Aunt Laura will be here."

The door opened, and her sister came into the room with a smug expression on her face. Kathleen wanted to scream in frustration.

"I'm here and Mom's gonna come up later. Now leave me alone with my favorite nephew," Laura said, gesturing for both Jared and Kathleen to go.

"I'm your only nephew."

"That doesn't mean you wouldn't be my favorite if I had twenty nephews."

"But that would mean I had twenty brothers!"

Jared tugged on Kathleen's hand. "Let's go and let them work it out."

There was a part of her that desperately needed to stay, to protect her heart, but for some insane reason her legs began to move and she soon discovered herself outside her son's room and being led out to Jared's car.

Settled in the passenger's seat, Kathleen finally found her voice. "Where are you taking me? Better yet, why are you here? I thought I made myself perfectly clear last night."

"You did. But I didn't. It's my turn to talk."

Kathleen crossed her arms over her chest. "Then talk so I can go back inside before my sister has my son convinced I need to have more children."

"Would that be so bad?"

Kathleen's mouth dropped open. Quickly she snapped it close and fumbled for the handle.

"I think I deserve the courtesy of you hearing me out. Please stay."

She sighed and released her grip on the door handle. "Okay but make it quick." *Before I lose my resolve and fling myself at you.*

He started the car.

Panic bolted through Kathleen. "Where are we going?"

"It's a surprise."

He tossed her a crooked grin that flipped her stomach. Her resolve began to slip. "But —"

"Please, Kathleen."

The appeal in his expression tore down all her defenses. She nodded and turned her gaze away from his to peer out the side window.

Twenty minutes later her panic had a firm grip on her. Jared pulled into the parking lot at the marina where he kept his sailboat. She remembered her first official date with Jared and how wonderful the day had been sailing on the lake.

"Jared, don't you think it would be better for both of us if we don't go —"

He held up his hand to stop her flow of words. "Bear with me on this."

"But nothing has changed since last night."

"Everything has changed, Kathleen." He pushed open his door, then came around to assist her from the car.

When she stood, her legs trembled. With her gaze glued on the beautiful thirty-foot sailboat, she followed Jared down the pier. The light breeze off the water carried the scent of fall in the air. Trees with orange, red and yellow leaves lined the shore. A tern flew overhead, its call vying with the sound of the waves lapping against the various craft.

Jared hopped on board, then offered her his hand to help her onto the sailboat. For a few seconds she hesitated. Once she stepped on the boat, she would have committed herself to staying to the end and hearing what he had to say. Could she afford to? She wanted desperately to be his wife, but she wouldn't put him into a situation such as he had had with his first marriage. She wanted a partner, not a caregiver.

With a deep breath of the crisp fall air, she placed her hand within his and descended onto the cushioned seat that ringed the back of the craft. His intense gaze captured hers.

"It won't take me long to get under way."

She touched his arm to stop him from turning away. The second her hand clasped his she knew the action had been a mistake. She didn't want to let go.

With an effort born out of desperation, she released her grip and quickly brought her arm to her side. "Let's talk now."

He flashed her a grin. "I was hoping to get you out on the water where you'd have to listen to me to the end."

She couldn't resist his impish look. "I promise I'll listen to everything you have to say." She scanned the horizon. "Besides it won't be light that much longer."

"I know. I wanted you to see the sun set on the water. We didn't get to do that the last time we were here. It's breathtaking."

"I'm sure it is." With the yellow orb dipping toward the line of trees along the western shore, she didn't have a doubt the setting would be beautiful — romantic. Already various shades of orange and red tinted the sky, making it seem as though it was on fire.

He ran his fingers through his hair, then rubbed the back of his neck, rolling his shoulders, as though preparing himself for battle. "Then here goes." He inhaled a deep breath. "I love you, Kathleen Somers. And I think we can have a future together."

"Jared, the problem —"

He pressed two fingers into her lips to still her words. "No, listen to what I have to say, then you can talk."

She nodded, her mouth tingling where he had touched her, reminding her yet again of how much this man affected her.

"You were right. I was blaming myself for Alice's death and I was blaming myself for Mark's relapse. I used Mark's illness as my penance for not being able to help Alice. Remember when I told you why I became a doctor?"

She nodded, recalling the story of his younger brother and his death when he was a teenager. He had drowned in the lake and Jared had tried to revive him after pulling him out.

"I loved my little brother a lot. We were best friends as well as brothers. When I couldn't save him, I vowed I would become a doctor and protect all the people I cared about. I had forgotten that God has the ultimate control over life and death, not me. Last night I did a lot of thinking about my situation, about my life, about my feelings for you."

Before her legs gave out, Kathleen settled on the cushion, her heart beating double time. Jared sat next to her, leaving, she saw thankfully, some space between them.

"It isn't easy for me to admit that my faith in the Lord wasn't as strong as I had thought. My faith is what helped me through my brother's drowning and Alice's alcoholism and her death, but I didn't really turn myself over to the Lord totally. I put conditions on that faith, conditions that in the long run were impossible. When you believe in God, there should be no conditions. I learned that from you. These past few months that's how you've dealt with Mark's illness. You've put it in God's hands. You didn't beat yourself up over his relapse. You handled it the way it should have been dealt with." Jared paused, blowing out a breath of air as if he had held it through his explanation.

Emotions kept in check flooded Kathleen. She so wanted to believe Jared could move on and forget the past. But doubt nibbled at her blossoming hope. "I don't know what the future holds for Mark. He will need a lot of support. I'm learning more and more about schizophrenia and realize each case is different. There is no road map my son will predictably follow. I can't ask you to deal with that on a day-to-day basis."

He slid closer, leaving little room between them. Taking her hands in his, he smiled, a calm composure settling over him. "But that's what love is all about. Sharing our lives completely. Alice didn't want to share her life and her problems with me. She pushed me away. We weren't a team. As long as I'm a total part of your life, I can handle anything. I can't change the past, but I can change the way I deal with it." He captured her face in his hands and stared into her eyes. "I love you."

With the last spoken so ardently her doubts began to dim. Maybe it could work.

She wanted to believe that more than anything. "What about Hannah and Terry? This could be a lot to ask of them."

"Hannah assured me last night that she and Terry want us all to be a family. They know Mark is ill and want to help him. They love you as I do."

The grin that accompanied his declaration sent her heart racing even more. But still she had to ask, "Are you sure about this, Jared?"

"I have never been more sure of anything in my life. These past months with you have shown me what a real relationship can be like. Will you marry me, Kathleen? For better, for worse."

She leaned forward and grazed her lips across his. "How can I refuse? You have quite a persuasive argument."

He wound his arms around her and drew her close, covering her mouth with his. His light kiss evolved into a soul-bonding one that rocked her very foundation.

When he pulled back, resting his forehead against hers, he asked, "Then I can take that as a yes?"

"Yes." Then more loudly she said, "Yes. Yes. I love you, Jared Matthews, with all my heart."

He pressed her against his length. "Want

to go sailing with me? There isn't a better view of the sun setting."

"I'd go anywhere with you." Kathleen thought of one of her favorite stories in the Bible, Ruth. Family was everything and now she would have a new, larger family to love, but best of all she would have Jared to love. She would share with him the joys and pains of life.

Epilogue

"Come on, you two, let's hurry. I don't want to be late. We need to get a good seat." Hannah tugged on Kathleen's hand, trying to move her faster.

Which was nearly impossible, Kathleen thought, lumbering toward the front of the rec hall. Being over eight months pregnant made it hard to do anything quickly.

"Honey, why don't you go ahead and save us two seats?" Jared asked, his arm about his wife.

"Sure." Hannah hurried away.

"Thanks." Kathleen paused, arching her back to try and ease the dull ache throbbing in its lower reaches. "At least I won't be pregnant during the worst part of summer."

"Hannah can hardly wait."

"That makes two of us."

"Actually three."

She leaned into Jared, marveling at how her life had changed over the year and half she'd been married to him. He was her support, her other half. Having this baby was a testament to the deep love they shared.

"I think I see Hannah waving from the front. We'd better get moving or she'll come and get us." Kathleen started forward with Jared by her side.

When they reached the front row of chairs, Jared helped Kathleen to sit. A few minutes later the lights dimmed.

"Mark and Terry are the first act," Hannah whispered.

Kathleen settled back and got as comfortable as possible when carrying around an extra twenty-five pounds. The dull ache in her back persisted, but she was determined to ignore it so she could enjoy her son and Terry playing a duet on the guitars.

When the two appeared on stage, Jared reached over and covered her hand with his, lacing their fingers together. Mark would be a senior in the next school year and would graduate. He hadn't had a relapse in over a year and was staying on his medication. She was sure early detection of his illness had helped her son and was so thankful to Jared for that.

As the first notes of the song, "Yellow Submarine," by the Beatles sounded in the quiet hall, Kathleen peered at Jared and caught his gaze. The love that shone in his eyes still made her heart pound against her chest and her throat contract with emotions. She mouthed the words, "I love you," then returned her attention to the stage and her two sons.

When Mark and Terry strummed the last note, the audience erupted with loud clapping. Kathleen joined in as the two took their bows, Mark and Terry beaming.

"Terry is becoming quite good," she whispered to Jared.

"Thanks to Mark."

A warm gush saturated her seat. Kathleen sucked in a deep breath. "Oh, my."

"What's wrong?"

"My water just broke."

DEAR READER

What the Heart Knows is a story of hope and friendship. Kathleen comes to Crystal Springs, her life turned upside down with the death of her beloved husband. Her son is acting odd, and she knows something is wrong. Jared befriends her and promises to help her discover what is wrong with her son. Through this journey they find love for each other. Her renewed faith in the Lord gives her the hope she needs to deal with her son's illness and to help Jared find the peace he needs to move on in his life.

One of my favorite books of the Bible is the story of Ruth. It is a story of friendship and commitment, but it is also a story of hope. Ruth and Naomi don't give up hope, and in the end Ruth is given a precious gift — a husband and a son. When faced with a difficult illness, having hope is so important. Even though Kathleen's son has schizophrenia, I wanted to show there is hope in dealing with the illness. New medications are helping. Early detection is important. Support for the person with schizophrenia and the family is also paramount. There are organizations that can help. In the United States there is the National Institute of Mental Health (NIMH), National Mental Health Association (NMHA), National Alliance for Research on Schizophrenia and Depression (NARSAD) and National Alliance for the Mentally Ill (NAMI).

I love hearing from readers. You can contact me at P.O. Box 2074, Tulsa, OK 74101 or Mdaley50@aol.com.

May God bless you,
Margaret Daley

About the Author

Margaret Daley feels she has been blessed. She has been married thirty-three years to her husband, Mike, whom she met in college. He is a terrific support and her best friend. They have one son, Shaun, who married his high school sweetheart in June 2002.

She has been writing for many years and loves to tell a story. When she was a little girl, she would play with her dolls and make up stories about their lives. Now she writes these stories down. She especially enjoys weaving stories about families and how faith in God can sustain a person when things get tough. When she isn't writing, she is fortunate to be a teacher for students with special needs. She has taught for over twenty years and loves working with her students. She has also been a Special Olympics coach and participated in many sports with her students.